I was in his arms as a lover rather than a terrorized victim

He handled me roughly indeed. I murmured, "Please—" It did no good. He staggered off through a wall of solid water carrying me in his arms. My head was against his throat and his laboring heart thundered in my ear as I clung to him. He was sobbing and I recalled what I'd once heard; that in times of great stress, strong men, brave men, have been known to cry even while fighting at the height of their strength. However, I was left to discover for myself that other emotions can rise unbidden in such circumstances; alarming reactions such as sensuality. Such a feeling gripped me, totally new in my experience; a hot surge of erotic attraction that defied the chill of the rain and I was in his arms as a lover rather than a terrorized victim who had just missed death by inches.

APPRENTICE IN TERROR
Paulette Warren

A BERKLEY MEDALLION BOOK
published by
BERKLEY PUBLISHING CORPORATION

BERKLEY MEDALLION BOOKS are published by
Berkley Publishing Corporation
200 Madison Avenue
New York, N.Y. 10016

BERKLEY MEDALLION BOOK ® TM 757,375

Printed in the United States of America

Berkley Medallion Edition, SEPTEMBER, 1976

1

Weird and wonderful are the ways of chance. Also, they can be frightening. To be hurled abruptly from a safe, routine academic life into a mad world of jousting knights, reckless stunt fliers, and priceless art treasures can tend to untrack one's sense of reality, especially when such transitions come about with scant warning.

In my case, I suppose there was a clue of sorts, however vague. It came that June day in 1932 in the form of a curious note from Judson Conroy of 417 Central Park West there in Manhattan:

> My Dear Miss Spain:
> If convenient, and I truly hope it will be, could you call on me at three P.M. on Sunday afternoon at the above address?
> I am down with a broken leg and cannot move because I find crutches an abomination. . . .

Of course, I knew who Judson Conroy was. Anyone with even a mild interest in the art world would have known of him, and such was his rating in the field that the note could have been likened to a royal command.

Also, directed as it was to an obscure art teacher in a small Manhattan college, it could have been a mistake.

The note arrived on Wednesday, the day—in my routine existence—for dinner with Max Bowman. So I had a few days to wonder about it.

Max was an integral part of my quiet, patterned way of life at the time. My *rut*, it could have been reasonably called. Max was practical, level-headed, and competent. He was a thinker who merited respect because, during the whole of our three years together he had been predicting doom and misery for the nation, and there we were, bogged down in the worst depression ever visited upon a confused people.

Max and I had met at Cooper Union, where I was attending some lectures on the French Impressionists and he was taking a finance and management course. One evening on a bench there in Astor Place he offered me half of his sardine sandwich and told me I should get new heels on my shoes because they had worn down and were throwing my spine out of alignment. A visit to the shoemaker proved him right.

We started from there and progressed so casually that there wasn't even a kiss for three weeks. But whatever our romance lacked in fire it made up in comfortable companionship. Marriage was never discussed, because it was not a time for planning ahead—for survival, rather, to wait for prosperity, which was reported to be just around the corner.

Max and I had remained safe from bread lines and apple selling. I was teaching art appreciation at Davidson College, and Max ran a bookkeeping service for a string of clients too small to need full-time help.

I had an efficiency apartment on East Thirty-sixth Street, where Max arrived that Wednesday; prompt as usual. As I stepped from the lobby of the building into the street, I caught a flash of him jumping dangerously from a bus in mid-block and dodging his way to the curb as though coming to rescue me from a thug with a knife at my throat. He skidded to a halt and ran his eyes up and down my length before giving the standard greeting. "You look great."

2

My wardrobe was somewhat above standard, though possibly a little dated, because most of it was hold-over from less cautious times. But I doubt if Max ever noticed. His appreciation would have been the same if I'd come out draped in flour sacks.

He pecked me on the cheek and rattled his pocket, where the jingle of silver proved him ready for our usual Wednesday-evening meal. He then took my arm and escorted me to the Automat on Times Square, where I went immediately to the balcony to hold our corner table while Max deposited nickels and dimes and quarters and followed me, his tray loaded with our usual selections.

While waiting, I'd read Judson Conroy's note again, and I handed it to Max when he was seated. As he read it, I asked myself some questions. Was I bored with Max? Was he bored with me? Were we being stupid, waiting for times to change before going on with our lives?

From what I could gather, the active generations of that period were reaching for whatever brass rings were offered, and while Max and I were hardly teenagers, the middle twenties was not exactly ancient. All over Manhattan—all over the country—speakeasies were doing booming business. Hip flasks were as common as wallets, and Prohibition was looked upon as pretty much of a joke.

The note from Judson Conroy, a break in my dull routine, no doubt sparked my sudden discontent and generated reckless questions. Suppose, that night, I were to say to Max: *Darling, let's not wait. Let's go upstairs and go to bed*. What would have been his reaction?

Unthinkable, of course. Max had seen me in my robe

3

on Sunday mornings when he came for coffee but had never requested that I remove it, nor had I ever suggested it.

How much of life, I wondered, was passing us by?

All of which was a great deal to go through my mind while Max set out my chicken a la king, my pickled beets, and my slice of lemon pie—these, of course, being my "usual."

"Who's Judson Conroy?" he asked.

"He runs the most prestigious art gallery on Fifty-seventh Street."

"Do you think he might need a bookkeeper?"

"I doubt it."

"What does he want to see you about?"

"I haven't the least idea."

"Why don't you phone him and find out?"

"I don't think I should appear overeager. I don't know what he wants."

"That's why you'd call—to ask him."

"I think I'd better wait."

"Okay. How about a walk up to Central Park? It's a nice evening."

Max showed no further interest, so we dropped the subject and I listened for the rest of the evening to Max's thoughts on the economy. Franklin Roosevelt, the ex-governor of New York, was running for president. Max liked some of his ideas. Others did not impress him. If given enough time, he thought Hoover might pull us out. And so on. . . .

Back on Thirty-sixth Street I invited him up for coffee, but he had some work to do on a couple of accounts. The good-night kiss was a little longer, with a shade more affection involved, but nothing to stir the passion. Upstairs, and somewhat in the dumps, I wondered if we were possibly wrong for each other. Or maybe I just didn't have what it took to raise the male blood pressure.

I showered and then checked that possibility by way of inspection in the mirror on my bathroom door. I looked all right to me. A quite decent figure: slim hips that showed no threat of broadening; legs to match; and a darkish complexion that did not redden in the sun. I had not changed greatly from my late teens, so all in all my body was about as *usual*. Maybe something else was wrong, perhaps the dictates of my karma insisting upon a prosaic life.

So I retired, and safe in my Murphy bed, which had only once reared up on its hind legs and threatened to pin me in the closet, my descent into self-pity continued in the form of fantasy.

Suppose, I told myself, the phone at my elbow would ring. Suppose the voice at the other end was that of a stranger, a male stranger, suggesting that we get together and break the moral code. How would I respond?

I would react with sophisticated amusement. I would reveal myself as modern-minded, unflappable, perfectly poised. Just distant enough, but not too distant.

The phone at my elbow jangled me out of my reverie.

I stared at it as though it were mocking me. Finally, after four rings, I picked it up and said hello.

"Hello, precious."

"Who is this?"

"The scourge of the flying circus, darling. The phantom himself at your service."

"You must have the wrong number."

"Oh, no. You *are* Karen Spain?"

"Yes, but—"

"I've been so wanting to hear your lovely voice."

"You're drunk, whoever you are."

The voice was unmistakably accented. An Englishman. Amused, sophisticated.

"I plead guilty, angel. Your American tonics are potent. I long for the taste of genuine Scotch that does not have to be frozen in ice cubes to swallow."

"You're disgusting. Drunk and calling a stranger at this hour of the night!"

"But it's early, lovely one. I am in a fantastic place with red plush drapes and cluttered furniture Jenny Lind would have loved. But Jenny, alas, is gone, so why don't you join me now instead of later?"

"If you'll tell me where you are, I'll call the police and send them for you."

It was all too unbelievable, as though some impish spirit had read my fantasy and now held me up to ridicule.

"You're disgusting!" I repeated. "And I refuse to lie here listening to your idiotic maunderings!"

"*Lie* there? Then you must be in bed. Upon my word! And not alone, I'm sure."

"Yes. Alone! If it's any of your business. Good *night*!"

I slammed the receiver down and fell back in complete confusion. Of all the colossal nerve! Some egocentric clown showing off in front of his sotted friends in some speakeasy! And why, out of all the girls in Manhattan, had he selected me to insult?

Gradually my anger ebbed, enough so that before I drifted off, my own thoughts came back to mock me. Amused, sophisticated, perfectly poised. Really!

All in all, it had been an exceptional day. . . .

2

Four-seventeen Central Park West, near 102nd Street, was one of those tall dignified buildings where the wealthy waited out the depression. A doorman led me to a closetlike elevator and punched the fifteenth-floor button before touching his cap and perhaps wishing me good luck, I wasn't sure. The lift crawled skyward, the door finally opening onto a tiny foyer with an apartment door on either side. The one bearing Judson Conroy's nameplate was partially open, with blaring music coming forth. A party was in progress, and I was forced to thread my way through a crowd as I entered.

The party had reached the uninhibited stage. A bald-headed man blew whiskey breath in my face as I passed and belched, "Lover! You've finally come!"

I moved on along a narrow hallway toward the front room, which appeared to be the center of activity. In the doorway, two young things, shapeless in their flowered shifts, faced each other in a frantic Charleston, hands flapping, knees banging.

The place was a museum of sorts, not exactly cluttered but containing far too much to classify quickly. Many of the pieces showed value at a glance. Others appeared to be more of personal and sentimental interest—a wall full of autographed pictures featuring Judson Conroy and various celebrities.

The party revolved around Conroy, who sat enthroned in the center of the huge room. His ailing leg in its bulky cast rested on a stool.

However, it was the throne which interested me more than the man. It was oriental in design, large enough to comfortably seat two persons. The gracefully curved back tiered from the center around to side panels in a half-circle. The lines were severe and functional, reflecting dignity rather than comfort. The entire surface of the piece was done in cloisonné of basic blue, tiny bits of enamel painstakingly assembled into flowered designs in which creative imagination and meticulous craftsmanship were perfectly blended. The magnificent piece glowed in royal splendor, making all else in the room look a little shabby.

I approached. A tall girl, all bones and slimness, paused to place a casual kiss on the top of Conroy's bald but well-shaped head, then drifted on. A small man arrived with a comment. His sharply pointed beard bobbed up and down as he spoke more with his chin than his lips.

Momentarily free, Conroy turned sharp blue eyes up at me. The face smiled but the eyes did not.

"Are you enjoying yourself, love?"

"Mr. Conroy?"

He shrugged amiably. "Who else?"

"I'm Karen Spain."

He was confused only for a moment. "Oh, yes."

"I got your note, but if the time isn't convenient for you . . ."

"But it is, dear. It's just that you're so prompt. Few people are, you know. Now, if you'll just hand me those abominable sticks . . ."

He indicated a pair of crutches on the floor by his throne. I picked them up as he lowered his gaily autographed cast to the floor with both hands and used my shoulder for support as he came erect.

"We can escape into the bedroom just there," he said, and began propelling himself toward a pair of French doors to the right. Humanity parted for him, and I trailed along like a small fish following in the wake of a whale.

Inside the room, a matched pair of guests, male and female, was stretched on the bed. There was little embarrassment, however, because their mood was more relaxed and conversational than passionate.

"Scat, children," Conroy ordered. "Close the door on the way out."

They left. Conroy said, "Now, if you'll just ease me into the window niche, you can use that chair, and we'll get to it." As I helped him, he chattered on in petulant complaint. "I was coming down from the balcony at the gallery. A circular staircase. I'd gone up and down a thousand times. Then the thousand and first did me in. The last step—the last one, mind you. I missed it, and didn't even fall—but there I was with a broken ankle. I just sat down on the floor and cursed like a longshoreman." His eyes never rested. They were like two bluebirds flitting from one twig to another. They rested upon me momentarily and turned piercing before they flitted on.

"You're quite attractive, my dear."

I thanked him while trying to appraise the rug under my chair. It was a sampler, early American primitive, with an alphabet worked in cross-stitch above a pastoral scene. It should not have been on the floor.

"I'm glad," he went on, "because I dislike ugliness in any form. So it follows that I am more at ease in the presence of beautiful people. Do you find that snobbish?"

9

"Mr. Conroy, I think you're just trying to make *me* feel more at ease."

He ignored that as he regarded me thoughtfully. "So you're the girl," he murmured.

"I don't understand . . ."

"The girl who embarrassed the Metropolitan Museum."

"Oh, *that!*"

The annoyance with which I reacted was sincere, but it did not bother him. He smiled—with his eyes this time.

"Tell me about it. Give me the first-hand story."

Bowing to his insistence, I went into a quick recounting of what had happened some months earlier at the museum. I was there with a class from the school, and being on familiar ground from many visits, I noticed a new acquisition in one of the galleries. I studied it for a few moments, and then we moved on. I met an assistant curator just outside the gallery. I knew him from previous visits, and after we'd exchanged greetings and a comment or two, I made the observation I was to regret: "By the way, that new Rembrandt in the Gide Collection, *Girl with Tulips*. It's a fake."

He smiled, and that was that, or so I thought. A week later, the scandal broke—a small one, with the public not greatly interested, but the discovery of the counterfeit made waves in the inner circles.

The distressing part came when I was given credit for the discovery and was interviewed by a *New York Times* reporter.

"You were quite vague when you talked to him, dear. So we never really found out. Now you must tell me. How did you·identify the painting as a forgery at a mere glance?"

10

"I didn't, really. It was just something that appeared to be a minor flaw. The ring Rembrandt's model was wearing. It was identical with one in a Sir Joshua Reynolds portrait done many years later. That did not necessarily prove the portrait a forgery. It just seemed odd, and when I called the painting a fake, I was not speaking seriously."

Conroy chuckled. "And the Reynolds turned out to be a fake also. That ring was the forger's signature. Hilarious."

"Mr. Conroy, I'm sure you didn't ask me here to inquire about that incident."

"Not entirely, but it does have a bearing. An important one. It tipped things in your favor for an assignment I have in mind for you."

"Then I'm sure you would want to know more about me than that."

"Oh, I do, my dear. I know much more. You are Karen Marcia Spain, twenty-five years old. You were born in Lewiston, Idaho, and came to New York to study art on a scholarship right after high school. Your parents were divorced, after which your father married again and went to South America. Your mother died five years ago. You have a married sister in California. You have been pretty much on your own since you left Idaho. You have a master's in fine arts. And your talents are probably being wasted as an art-appreciation teacher at Davidson College."

All that knowledge of me and my affairs was disturbing. What right had he to snoop so exhaustively?

"You've been thorough," I said. "It certainly was not from mere curiosity."

"Hardly. I need someone to do a job for me—to

11

negotiate some purchases. I'm offering you the assignment."

"Purchases of what?"

"Art objects. Possibly a million dollars' worth."

I could not suppress a gasp. "But why me? I'm an art teacher, not an appraiser. I've had no experience."

"For two reasons, my dear. You are honest, and you're an expert. Whether you've had any practical experience or not, you know values in the field. No one could push shoddy material off on you."

"But . . ."

He was obviously enjoying my surprise. He said, "My dear, every successful professional in any field had to be trusted by someone. And that's my specialty. I discover talent and put it to work."

"But . . . a million dollars! To be trusted . . ."

His restless gaze paused again to peer. "Miss Spain, when you arrived, I noticed that you gave special attention to my chair. What was your verdict?"

I replied out of my confusion, without thought. "Chinese. From the Imperial Palace in Jehol, I think. A fine example of that period's craftsmanship."

"The finest. If I were auctioning it off, what would you offer?"

"That would depend on the competition and who was supporting my bid. One of the great national museums might go to a million and a half. There is a chair just like it in the Ethnographic Collection at Oslo University."

"Then you didn't realize that mine is a duplicate?"

"I suspected as much, but I would have to examine it more closely to be sure. It is the sort of piece where duplication can produce equal excellence. Only the age and authenticity of the original makes it priceless."

12

He seemed highly pleased with my reply, but as I suspected, more pleased with himself.

"All right, now let me tell you about the assignment I have for you. Did you ever hear of a man named Jasper King?"

"A collector, I believe. A Texas oil man. I haven't heard of him recently."

"King always was an eccentric, and he did drop out of sight. He was lucky in oil and went up like a rocket. But then he came down again—speaking comparatively, that is. King, along with many others, guessed wrong in the stock market. The rebound that he expected never came. His cash and assets have been wiped out, except for many of his art treasures. His needs are now desperate. This isn't public knowledge, you understand. But I happen to know that a few bundles of hard cash would tempt him sorely."

This was becoming more unbelievable with every passing moment. "*That* would be my assignment? To buy Jasper King's art collection?"

"To try, my dear. To try. You won't find them sitting on counters with price tags attached. And you may fail. But I have a feeling you just might do it."

"I certainly appreciate your confidence in me. . . ."

"You merit that confidence. My instincts tell me so. But of course there are other factors involved. I can't go myself because King knows me personally and despises me. I outbid him on a Cellini goblet a few years ago. He wanted it very badly and claimed that I used unethical tactics."

"Did you?" I asked the question suddenly, feeling a recklessness that seemed to go with the time and the place.

"Certainly. And I don't demand that you be honest

with anyone but me. As a safeguard, I'll pay you enough in salary and bonuses to make honesty well worth your while."

"I just don't know what to say, Mr. Conroy."

"Then just say yes." He sighed. "I envy you the experience you're going to have. One enchantment after another, I suspect."

"Honestly, Mr. Conroy, I'm long past understanding you." That was hardly true. I was closer to understanding him than before, or at least thought so. Below the surface, he was practical and as hard as nails; to an extent, I felt that his belief in me was bolstering my faith in myself. But on the surface he enjoyed showmanship and milked every scene for as much drama as possible. I now saw that the adulation of the noisy crowd outside was important to his ego. Curiously, I felt a little sorry for him. He was solid enough in his success not to need the superficial.

"As I said," he went on, "Jasper King always was an eccentric, but now he seems to be reaching beyond that. He retired from the world, way up on the New England coast, into a weird castle built by a crazy Englishman some eighty or ninety years ago. He moved in there and surrounded himself with all his treasures after they abused him outrageously in the stock market. It's as though he's daring the world to come and get him. Only very selected guests are allowed on the premises. Poor old Jasper, I'm afraid, has gone well off his trolley."

I had to admit my disappointment. "Then you've given me an impossible assignment. You say he despises you, and I'm hardly a selected guest. I probably wouldn't be allowed past his front gate."

"Hardly a gate, my dear. A moat. Honestly. It's a

14

real castle, complete with a moat and a drawbridge and parapets for Hamlet's father to prowl about on at night.''

"Then it's even worse. Hopeless, wouldn't you say?''

That annoyed him. "Miss Spain, in that case, would I have taken up your time by inviting you here?''

"I suppose not. . . .''

"You will be delivered into the enemy's bastion. Your only problem will be how you conduct yourself after you get there.''

Conroy's overblown language did not bother me so much as the implication of what he said—making the assignment sound more like an invasion of a hostile realm than a commission to buy art.

"You will represent a syndicate,'' he went on, "and you won't be necessarily deceiving King, because I am a member of that syndicate. I have financial backing in this operation. It's just that you mustn't be associated with me personally in any way.''

"I refrain from mentioning your name, is that it?''

"Exactly. I'll brief you further on procedure. But first I must have your word one way or another. Do you accept or reject?''

"Must I decide at this moment?''

"I'm afraid so, Miss Spain. The time is short. Secrets of this sort are not kept indefinitely. There are others who covet the treasures up there.''

Curiously, my reluctance was more academic than personal. The promise of change, excitement, new vistas weighed heavily in Conroy's favor—this somewhat to my surprise, because I had not completely realized my own restlessness. The offer certainly sparked my need to get out of the rut I was in. However, there were the times. A nation on its financial back, so to speak. Men were selling apples in the street. Others who had held good jobs were now standing in line for a snatch of food. Captains of finance and industry were jumping from windows. So it was hard for me to conceive that such men as Judson Conroy still existed—awesomely wealthy; talking in terms of millions; seemingly unaware that a single dollar was looked upon by others as an impossible goal.

Conroy seemed to be divining my thoughts. Speaking more softly, he said, "My dear, civilization does not stop because the economy goes slightly out of gear from time to time. Depressions are opportunities for some and disaster for others. Which side do you prefer?"

The argument was most persuasive. It left only the first question that had flashed into my mind.

Why me?

I answered in wordless evasion. Conroy had given me his reasons. If he used bad judgment, it was his mistake, not mine. And with all factors considered, the proposition now loomed as an opportunity in a time when opportunities were seldom presented. In my confusion and uncertainty, one fact loomed clearly: if I walked away from Conroy's offer, I would spend the rest of my life berating myself for timidity.

So, attempting to speak firmly, I said, "Very well, Mr. Conroy. I'm your girl."

The phrasing amused him. It brought a twinkle into his eyes as he glanced ruefully at his cast.

"But only up to a certain point, I'm sure."

"Of course." Perhaps I reddened a little.

He rubbed his hands together as though the project

16

had already succeeded. "Fine. You are able to move immediately, I hope."

It came as a kind of shock that there was nothing of importance to hold me. That did not seem right. It bothered me to realize that my roots were so shallow, that I could vanish from Manhattan with others perhaps curious as to what had happened to me but in no way vitally concerned. There was Max, of course. He would be concerned, but I had no obligation to him. In essence, I was free as a bird.

A lonesome bird?

Only now did I realize clearly that I had led too narrow a life, and here was a golden opportunity to broaden it.

"We'll have a final briefing in the morning, my dear. Then you will leave for the battleground."

Again that disturbing implication—a war rather than a peaceful mission. "As I said—"

"I know. You're my girl. And now, if you'll help an old cripple back to his throne, we'll go on with the party."

There was one more incident there on Judson Conroy's premises before I left, minor but most indicative. After I had piloted Conroy back to his Chinese chair, a man approached me. First impressions ticketed him in my mind as being handsome as sin. He had a shock of yellow hair, his whole image shouting glamour. Slim in the hips, broad in the shoulders, he lifted a champagne glass and gave me a smile that suggested warm secrets between us.

Conroy introduced us tersely while his gaze swept the party as though to see if anyone was missing. "Jeff Stone, Karen Spain," he said with a quick gesture.

"Hi, love."

The tone was as warm as the smile. Yet, I thought, faintly contemptuous.

"Mr. Stone," I acknowledged.

Judson Conroy cut in. "Jeff, get me a drink—the Scotch that just arrived."

The man obeyed, but slowly, with a sort of controlled arrogance, a reaction, no doubt, to the sharpness of Conroy's order. He resented it but could not defy the master. I wondered about Conroy's coldness and decided it was merely characteristic.

But Jeff Stone was more centered in my mind. Deciding that these feverish pleasure-seekers were outside my orbit, I moved toward the door, into the claustrophobic little elevator, and down into the street. In a sense, Jeff Stone went with me. The breeches of military cut; the highly polished boots; the loose shirt collar stuffed with an artfully tied yellow scarf.

But mainly, the voice. I'd heard it before—over my phone the previous night. And curiously, it was Jeff Stone who symbolized the sinister aspects of my assignment rather than the more tangible dangers of what Judson Conroy had told me.

It was Jeff Stone whose smile, leer, and soft voice suggested forces moving in on me. . . .

3

I should have called Max that very night. I did not, no doubt because of a divided mind; the committed part seemed to be dragging the still-reluctant half along on a leash, and I was afraid Max would talk me out of my mad adventure.

So I waited until after the final briefing I received the next morning in Conroy's apartment, then phoned Max and suggested dinner. He knew it was something special, because that was my wash night.

In a generally defiant mood, I vetoed the hard reality of the Times Square Automat in favor of a small French restaurant on Thirty-fourth Street where there were candles and soft music. This may have sprung from guilt, a desire to ignite a spark between us before it was too late.

He was more curious than romantic and listened with interest as I brought him up-to-date.

"It sounds like a real opportunity," he said.

There was a wistfulness in his voice that encouraged me.

"The assignment will take me away from New York. And from what I can gather, I'll be completely out of touch."

"You can send a postcard once in a while . . . and it isn't forever."

"That's true."

"You can call it a vacation."

"I suppose I could."

"And the money. Where else could you pick up several thousand dollars in times like these?"

"Honestly, Max, the money is secondary. I'm getting along fine as it is. My salary is adequate, my job is secure."

"You talk as though money were unimportant. Nobody has security these days. Your school could close tomorrow."

My hand had been under his, but now he withdrew to lift his coffeecup. "You didn't tell me how you're supposed to get to that ridiculous place."

"By air."

"By air! What's Conroy doing—chartering a plane?"

"I don't really know. Something came up that he had to attend to this morning while we were talking, so all he told me was to take a cab to Newark airport tomorrow morning. I'm to be there at nine o'clock. I'm to go to Gate Three."

The waiter arrived with our check. It was eight dollars, and I felt that I should pay it, because the restaurant had been my idea. At the last moment, however, I considered Max's pride and held off.

We walked hand-in-hand back to my apartment, which was encouraging. Then Max refused an invitation to come up.

"You've got things to do. Packing, getting ready."

I was clearly aware at that moment of the barrier between us. Max's pride. It was a basic characteristic, not something that flared at intervals. He was the kind of man who would take nothing to which he was not entitled. In the plainest of terms, he had never taken me because by his standards he could not afford me. By

20

those same standards, we were now farther apart than ever.

Therefore, knowing his kiss would be the merest peck, I took charge and went into his arms with a frank determination to stir his lust if there was no other way. I pressed hard against him, found his mouth, and opened my lips to his. It was a wonderfully wanton feeling, a reckless tearing aside of inhibitions. For a long moment, he responded; and to the extent possible under those circumstances, there in the doorway, I gave him my body—or at least, the promise of it.

He refused.

And because it was an act the nature of which hinged totally upon the result achieved, it was a failure even to the point of making me feel cheap. He was human and he wanted me, but against the wall of his pride it became a taunt, a shallow offering of what he needed so terribly but could not take.

As he drew away, my tears were close to the surface. I whispered, "Good-bye, Max. I'll write," and rushed inside, where an unsuspected depth of emotion exploded in sobs of misery and frustration. How on earth, I stormed inwardly, could one person be so inadequate!

Upstairs, I plunged into packing the single suitcase I would take. Then, achieving a comparative calm, I prepared for bed and lay wide-eyed in the darkness.

Only then did I acknowledge the truth I'd been too cowardly to face—that while in Max's arms my thoughts had been of that handsome, arrogant face beneath the shock of yellow hair.

I'd kissed Max while thinking of Jeff Stone. . . .

4

An attendant was standing at Gate Three at Newark airport. It was my first visit to such a place, though I'd read that the development of air travel was one of the great hopes of a crippled economy; there had been a visionary article about a future in which great airliners would transport hundreds of passengers across land and ocean faster than the speed of sound. Visionary, but hopeful.

The airport consisted mainly of one-story wooden buildings with larger Quonset-type sheet-metal structures to house the planes. Several of the larger ones were out on runways, and one was being boarded by a line of passengers. I wondered where the plane was bound and wished the passengers a safe journey.

The attendant at the gate was middle-aged and red-faced. He looked to be a retired Irish policeman. He took my bag and in answer to his inquiring look I said, "I am Karen Spain. I was told to—"

"Oh, sure, miss. You're the colleen for the private plane yonder."

I had no way of knowing where "yonder" was until he led me off away from the commercial section to where several smaller aircraft were grouped—looking a little lonely beside the huge passenger planes nearby.

The attendant called out jovially, "Here she is, Mr. Stone. Your lady is right on time."

I should have known! Even at our first meeting, Jeff Stone's whole appearance had shouted airman. I should have known, and still I resented Judson Conroy not telling me.

Jeff Stone, white teeth ablaze, yellow hair attractively tousled, was posed glamorously against the propeller of a two-seated biplane, a beautiful hawklike thing. It was of bright silver with a red nose just behind the propeller and red fins at the rear; red tail feathers seemed more apt in my concept of a sleek bird waiting to make sport of gravity's silly law. The plane's whole aspect was exciting.

I was pleased also to see Jeff Stone's shell of arrogant sophistication at least temporarily broken. After his heavily anglicized, "Hi, love," he turned adoring eyes to the plane and patted its side.

"A Snipe," he said. "British. Bentley two-thirty horse. Twenty-thousand-foot ceiling. A hundred-twenty miles an hour. Three-hour endurance."

Here he paused apologetically. "Of course, that's not very fast, but she was built before the war and maneuvered right along with the best the Germans could show up with."

I was determined not to be impressed. "Three-hour endurance," I said. "Does that mean it falls to pieces if we stay up any longer?"

"It means, precious, that we can make our destination in one hop with a full tank."

"And I presume you're taking me with you."

"That's the general idea."

"All right. Which hole do I get into?"

"You ride in the forward cockpit. You'll have to take your suitcase in with you. There's no baggage space. I'll stow it for you."

He took my suitcase and climbed lithely up in a single movement, scorning the niche in the side of the

24

plane that corresponded functionally to the stirrup of a saddle.

"It's a good thing I didn't bring two suitcases," I said.

"We would have emptied one and stuffed the other. Now you, precious."

There was hardly time to tell him to stop calling me "precious." He turned me quite possessively to face the plane, then reached down and lifted one of my feet and guided it into the supporting niche. This was done by grasping my ankle quite high up on the calf and moving my leg with authority.

My protest was cut off: "I'm quite capable of—"

By that time I was being lifted, his other hand casually under my skirt and gripping the bare flesh of my middle thigh. As I went into the cockpit, there was no way to keep my skirt down, so he had to know that I wore pink underthings and my skin up to the edge of my chemise was unflawed.

"Sorry," he said casually, his arrogance back in place. "Clumsy of me."

That cut off the explosive protest on the tip of my tongue. A little late for indignation, I thought.

Stepping up on the wing, he brought forth a leather helmet. "Here, let me put this on you."

I snatched it from him. "I'm quite capable of dressing myself, thank you!"

That brought a grin—an aggravating implication that the secret we shared was now deeper than ever. As I clawed the helmet over my hair, I wondered how I could possibly have been attracted to this conceited lout. My indignation was of benefit, though. It crowded out the anxiety of a first trip off the ground in a fragile vehicle that depended only upon some sort of vacuum over its wings to keep it aloft—supported, in short, by nothing whatever.

I pouted over the assault against my modesty while Jeff donned his helmet, buttoned his leather jacket, and climbed into the cockpit behind me. An overalled individual had arrived from somewhere. Jeff called out, "Contact." The man answered by repeating the word and then threw his weight against the propeller. It spun a couple of times, the motor sputtered a complaint, and the attendant looked pensively at the uncooperative propeller.

The process was repeated twice more, and I was almost ready to climb out and demand less chancy transportation when the motor caught and roared and the propeller became a circular blur there in front of me.

Jeff taxied out onto a runway, where we waited for a big commercial plane to lumber into the sky. Then a wave from the tower nearby sent us on our way.

My first reaction was strong doubt. I don't know what I expected, but the sensation was hardly monumental. The motor roared joyfully, the wind tore past my screen, the beautiful Snipe glided up into the air, and all my fears of flying vanished. All I could think of was: how wonderful!

Thus I was able to enjoy a feeling of triumph as the Manhattan skyline turned into little toy buildings in some child's play yard. Even my resentment to Jeff Stone faded as I soaked up the pleasure of this new experience.

We were following the coastline north, and nothing untoward happened for an hour or so. I had come to a point where the novelty of that small world below had worn off. Then, quite suddenly, the drone of the motor turned into a cough and faded. The sudden silence was deafening as the nose of the plane dipped downward. Wind whined through the wings.

"Are you enjoying yourself?"

It was Jeff's voice calling out. I turned in panic and saw his goggled face. I'd lowered the goggles attached to my helmet, and for moments we goggled at each other while I sought to cry out but was unable.

"It would be more fun," he called, "if someone was up here trying to shoot us down."

"What happened?" I managed to scream. "Are we going to crash?"

"We're just gliding. No problem."

"Well, *stop* it!"

He grinned and pulled up the Snipe's nose. The motor responded. The propeller went back to work, and I raged in my soul at Jeff Stone for putting me through that trauma. He was a sadist who enjoyed seeing people suffer. I wondered how many wings he'd pulled off flies in his childhood.

The plane droned on through the second hour of our journey. It was then that the sky began to darken. A gust of wind from the north fluttered the Snipe's wings in sudden petulance. The laboring motor snarled bravely, and the propeller seemed to claw at the air to keep itself aloft.

Jeff changed course, in away from the ocean, and I saw towering above us a great bank of black clouds. How had I missed them? From whence had they come so suddenly?

I sensed Jeff's concern, then craned my neck about, to see narrowed eyes behind his goggles. A slash of lightning tore the sky, and a few moments later the thunder reached us, a sound of bowling balls crashing into giant pins.

Oddly, I was less panicky with real danger facing us than before, when Jeff's cute trick with the controls had put my heart into my mouth; perhaps because here there was forewarning. The whole threatening sky spread out above me. It was a matter of facing the inevitable. What would be would be.

The sound of the Snipe's motor rose and fell as the plane struggled with the increasing turbulence of the elements. Then the seat seemed to drop out from under me, jerking my seat belt hard against my body, and the plane went straight down. Not in a nose dive; instead, it suddenly changed levels, the way an elevator would fall if the cable were suddenly cut. Then it jerked to a thudding stop, as though that same elevator had hit bottom.

We had dropped through an air pocket and come down hard enough to rattle my teeth. My reaction was a kind of childish petulance rather than fear. All the fuss and bother for nothing: Judson Conroy's offer; my acceptance; the packing and the excitement—only to come to this ridiculous end.

My prayer was curious also: Let's get this over with while I can still stave off screaming panic.

We were in the heart of the storm now, in a black, howling turbulence that flung the plane around like a kite with a broken string. It was a paradox that, while the seconds seemed to drag into minutes, there was still only time to regret a past sin or two and relive quick flashes of my yesterdays. I thought of Max, of the swing in our backyard at home with one rope slightly longer than the other. My father had vowed to fix it, but he never did. Peggy's agonized confidences when she found herself in trouble. *A baby. Oh, my God! He's got to marry me, Karen! He must!* And just in time, too. Happy in California? Should have written oftener. Too late now. . . .

We crashed. . . .

5

There was a clanging of metal outside my window.

It started faintly, as of faraway bells, then increased to a discordant racket as I awakened.

I opened my eyes. I was in a bed of regal proportions, and what with the room around it, my first thought was unique. This was a place of royalty—where princelings were born to be reared in splendor and to rule great nations. The bed, a four-poster, was on a platform, the canopy bordered in looped red satin with black tassel trim. There were drapes of a lighter satin material that had not been drawn, and I looked out at a far wall where four lancet windows ran to the height of the fifteen-foot vaulted ceiling. I had not died. I had merely retrogressed into the Middle Ages.

It was not a case of returning from any great gap in consciousness. While I could not remember the room, there was a chain of recall reaching back over the preceding hours, sketchy in places, and with some gaps, but coherent enough to remind me that my arrival at Caliban's Castle had been little short of spectacular.

Acting on the basis of first things first, I closed my eyes, ignored the metal hammering outside, and tried to relive the immediate past.

The progression had, to begin with, the sensation of being a tennis ball bouncing along a court overgrown and abandoned. That was when the gallant little Snipe, answering to Jeff Stone's commands, did the best it could. Finding smooth ground in the rough country below us had been impossible, so with time having run

31

out, Jeff brought the plane down in an area of growth less theatening than that around it. The trees were on the sapling side, and the undergrowth into which we plunged acted as a cushion, and we bounced several times in tooth-loosening fashion. I'd braced myself as much as I was able, but with the propeller already bent out of shape, I was sure the motor would land in my lap before we could come to whatever halt was in store for us.

We terminated with a thud, slamming my head against the cowling around the upper edge of the cockpit. It was padded, but I was still knocked unconscious.

It was only vaguely that I could recall being hauled from the plane, but I was conscious of Jeff Stone's frantic concern. He handled me roughly indeed. I murmured, "Please . . ." It did no good. As he dragged me out of the cockpit like a sack of meal, he gasped, "Even with the rain, she could still explode!"

He was the expert, but I still could not see how any form of fire could have prevailed in that torrential downpour. He staggered off through a wall of solid water, carrying me in his arms. My head was against his throat, and his laboring heart thundered in my ear as I clung to him. He was sobbing, and I recalled what I'd once heard—that in times of great stress, strong men, brave men, have been known to cry even while fighting at the height of their strength. However, I was left to discover for myself that other emotions can rise unbidden in such circumstances, alarming reactions, such as sensuality. Such a feeling gripped me, totally new in my experience, a hot surge of erotic attraction that defied the chill of the rain; and I was in his arms as a lover rather than a terrorized victim who had just missed death by inches.

A few moments later, Jeff kicked open a door, and we were inside. Storm clouds had brought gray twilight, leaving just enough light to show that our sanctuary was bare, empty of furniture. That did not bother me in the least. The roof was rainproof, and the feel of the solid floor under me as Jeff eased me down was cause for thanksgiving.

Totally exhausted, Jeff fell across me. "Are you hurt?"

"I don't think so," I replied.

"God! You could have been killed."

"We were lucky."

"You must be frozen. . . . Hold tight," he said, and got up and went into the next room, and I discovered that I was wrong about the cottage being bare of furnishings. He returned with a chair and a footstool, which he began smashing into kindling against the stone wall of the fireplace.

"Thank heaven the drapes are still here. You might pull them down while I start a fire."

I pulled the drapes off their rods, feeling no better than a vandal. I carried them back to the fireplace, where Jeff was nursing a small flame.

"All right," he now commanded, "out of those wet clothes and dry off." When I hesitated, his voice sharpened. "Let's not be coy. This is hardly a romantic setting. Or do you want me to do it?"

"Never mind," I replied, and began getting out of the icy garments that promised me pneumonia if I did not hurry.

"I'll find some more fuel," Jeff said, and moved off into other parts of the cottage. By the time he returned, I was less of an icicle. The rough monk's cloth of the drapes served excellently to rasp the blood back from where it had been hiding in the marrow of my bones. Jeff returned with another chair. He regarded me critically. "Better?"

"Much," I replied from the very edge of the now-blazing fire. Its warmth plus the drape I'd wrapped myself in were serving me quite well.

"Careful you don't set yourself on fire," Jeff warned as he stripped to the waist and began looking to his own comfort.

A wave of shame and uncertainty swept me. That totally unfamiliar surge of erotic surrender while he'd carried me in his arms. A comparative stranger. Did that reveal that I was possessed of a shallowness I had never suspected?

However, my psyche—or whatever part of one receives the brunt of such censure—refused to hang its head. Buoyed up, no doubt, by the feeling of having been recalled to life, I regarded the fine lines of Jeff's naked torso and savored the memory of that physical contact. Even in the harsh environment through which we had struggled, I had felt safe and protected. And that sweet feeling of surrender had been no coy maidenly dream. But there *was* a sense of having cheated good, faithful Max. Had the shallowness of our romance been my fault or his?

Jeff now wrapped a drape around his shoulders and dropped cross-legged beside me. The firelight brushed his profile with light and shadow, and if he had chosen to kiss me at that moment, he would have encountered no resistance. He had called this an unromantic situation and had evidently meant it. His mood was now somber, almost sullen, possibly because of our close brush with death.

"Welcome to Caliban's Castle," he said.

"Thank you. But I did expect something a little more elaborate."

"This is a cottage out on the edge of the estate. It's a whale of a layout; wild, unimproved, most of it. I was damned lucky. I came down in familiar territory, even if I wasn't able to reach the flats. The castle itself is about four miles east of us."

"I don't understand the name. The place belongs to Jasper King, doesn't it? Who is Caliban?"

"Caliban Leach. An English lord. He dates back almost a hundred years. So does the castle."

Unimportant, really, but it struck a discord. It made me realize how little I knew about the whole operation, as though I were being led blindfolded into mysterious places.

Jeff appeared to sense my thought. He said, "Angel, don't take things too seriously. Sending you up here was a wild shot on Judson Conroy's part. Something that *might* work. All he knows for sure is that King needs money and you know art. He knows you're reliable and that you wouldn't overpay."

"He's certainly taking a lot for granted."

"Hardly. Jud does have an instinct for people."

"The Barlow Syndicate I represent. Does it actually exist?"

"Oh, yes. In fact, I own a small piece of it. For services rendered, you might say."

Tell me, Jeff—exactly who are you? I think I have a right to know."

He had pretty well recovered from the shock of our experience. The arrogant self-assurance I instinctively resented was now returning. I had certainly liked him better the other way. Which, I wondered, was the true man?

His expression turned reflective. "A good question, pet. Who is Jefferson Hardwick Stone? Sometimes I wonder myself."

"You were a flyer in the World War?"

"The Royal Air Force. Early. The Gray Ghost Squadron. I joined as soon as I could lie convincingly about my age—when all we had were a few Camels against Richthofen's Flying Circus. Our guns jammed half the time. But there was always enough brandy to toast those who didn't come back." His emotion deepened as he fell to quoting: " 'This blessed plot, this earth, this realm, this England . . .' Forgive me, angel. It was a long time ago."

I could not help but be moved by his fervor, even though it seemed somewhat overemotional for the time and the place.

"Since then I've been blown by the winds of fortune. Here . . . there. . . . You might say I've lived on borrowed time and lived to the hilt."

All very impressive, but it did not answer my questions. I said, "You're obviously a close friend of Judson Conroy's. And you must also know Jasper King."

He laughed. "A great pair to draw to. Judson's a lucky fool, and Jasper is mad as a hatter."

"I was told that they despise each other."

"Ha! Give them knives, they'd cut each other to bits. You understand that you aren't to mention Conroy's name."

I suddenly wondered what madness on my part had made me accept this crazy mission. "I do. But what I don't understand is why Jasper King should accept me on any terms."

"Because he needs money."

"That's ridiculous! It should make him even more

suspicious. It has no bearing on my credentials . . . or lack of them.''

''No problem there, sweet. You're coming in as my bird.''

''Your *bird*! What on earth are you talking about?''

''My girl. The love of my life. The beautiful wench with whom I shall pass the rest of my years.''

I was stunned, so shocked that I reacted physically, and the drape I was clutching almost fell from my shoulders to my lap, which would have left me exposed from the waist up.

''Beautiful,'' he murmured.

I snatched the drape back into place, struggling at the same time to hold my anger in check. There was no point in going into a tantrum. Gritting my teeth, I counted to ten under my breath.

''You and Judson Conroy made only one mistake,'' I said. ''An important one. You withheld important facts. That lapse negates the whole plan. I'll be returning to the city as soon as I can find transportation.''

He shrugged, his smile remaining. ''I told Jud you weren't the type. Too straitlaced. A pity. Now my commission goes down the drain. And I'm broke, precious, I haven't a shilling. The Snipe is smashed. How are the soup kitchens back in Gotham?'' He reached out boldly and neatened the drape around my shoulders, drawing it up more firmly in a gesture of finality.

I said, ''So the whole operation was a confidence game. You plan to impose upon your friendship with Jasper King in order to betray him to Judson Conroy, with me as the instrument of betrayal.''

''I *could* resent that, precious. . . .''

''Will you stop using those endearing names?''

''Of course, pet, but you implied cheating, stealing

37

Jasper's worldly goods through subterfuge. Not the case. Not the case at all. You weren't asked to make unfair bids. We aren't passing Judson's precious artworks out the window in the dead of night. We are merely finding our way around his eccentric barriers to free trade.''

It was a novel argument. It put the thing in a somewhat different light. Then the discussion was adjourned abruptly when someone pounded on the door, opened it, and peered in. A man in boots and a slicker, with a less than cordial welcome.

''Who are you? What are you doing here?''

6

The search party that tracked the crashed plane and found us in the cottage set the mood for our reception. Hostile. Suspicious.

After Jeff identified us, we were grudgingly given transportation to the castle headquarters of Jasper King, who was fast becoming an unsubstantiated rumor in my mind rather than a person.

Deep gloom now permeated everything. The storm clouds had passed over, but twilight set in swiftly as we were driven over a winding, rutty road in a wagon drawn by a team of horses, a crude four-wheeled vehicle that could easily have passed as a prison wagon. A pair of silent outriders flanked us, and regardless of having been informed by Jeff that I'd come as his *bird*—his mistress or what-have-you—I was grateful for his presence by my side, the warm grip of his hand, and the pressure of his thigh against mine.

Nothing happened to lessen the macabre aspects of our arrival. After a bone-jarring ride of some miles, I saw just ahead—against the darkened eastern sky—the silhouette of Caliban's Castle. If I could have been transported at least psychologically into medieval England I might have seen the place as sanctuary. As things stood, it was quite the opposite. The great, brooding pile looked for all the world like a Doré illustration out of Dante's *Inferno*.

This impression was heightened by a phenomenon of which I had not been informed. A huge cloud of flame-tinted smoke rising above it told me that the place was on fire.

"Jeff!" I gasped. "My God!"

He drew me into the circle of his arm. "It's all right, angel. I didn't get a chance to tell you about the thermal fault."

"I don't understand."

"The castle sits squarely upon a hole in the ground— although it's hardly that. A geological split in the earth that allows heat to rise. The temperature inside stays around eighty-nine degrees winter and summer. There's a tropical garden inside the walls. You'll be enchanted."

Shivering there in his arms, enchantment was the last thing I could visualize. "But the smoke . . . the flame!"

"Steam, precious, not smoke. The inner square of the castle is open, and when the cold rain hits the heated area, things fog up a bit. Jasper installed a dynamo. The lights give that look of flame down below."

It was too much. Terror and weariness had drained me, and I was on the verge of hysteria. My imagination ran wild: None of this was real. I was trapped in an impossible theatrical production staged for the amusement of the gods. The things I beheld were stage props, and soon we would all descend into hell for the final scenes and the climax, with evil triumphant over good.

The wagon rattled across what later turned out to be the drawbridge over a moat, and so I did not see much of what was inside, because I gave up the ghost, so to speak. I fainted in Jeff's arms.

And now, here I was—back in the land of the living, daylight streaming in the windows, my suitcase open nearby, and my brand-new yellow silk nightgown coming into view as I sat up in bed. Jeff had no doubt carried me from the wagon to this preposterous bedroom. Had he also prepared me for bed and tucked me in?

I remembered his revelation concerning what our relationship would be in Jasper King's eyes, and I looked quickly at the pillow next to mine there on the bed. It had not been used.

That was a great relief. At least, I told myself it was a great relief, and instantly banished the absurd idea that there was even a tinge of disappointment.

A renewed clanging of metal caught my attention. That racket from somewhere outside. I got out of bed and went to a window.

Again that sense of unreality took over, the feeling of retrogression, because out there on the lawn beyond the moat, two knights in full medieval armor were slashing at each other with broadswords. They were in classical contrast. The white knight gleamed in aluminum brightness, the sun glinting and dancing off his regalia, while his opponent in dull black perhaps represented the forces of evil come to take the castle.

There were spectators who did not appear to care which side won so long as brisk action continued—half a dozen beautifully costumed ladies seated at two tables under fringed pastel umbrellas who clapped and enthused when the contest erupted into spasms of heightened violence.

My first thought was how long it must have taken those ladies to get into their costumes; the vast skirts supported by petticoat after petticoat; the wasped-in, high waistlines that accentuated tightly bodiced bosoms at each breath. They were King Arthur-authentic, even to the tall peaked hats with varicolored streamers adding gaiety and grace to the scene. . . .

"As I said, Jasper is eccentric."

I whirled and managed to croak, "Do you have to scare a person to death?"

Jeff Stone stood there holding my robe in his hands. He did not apologize. "I suppose you'll want to put this on."

The regret in his voice was a compliment, my nightgown highly revealing there in the bright sunlight. I slipped into the robe and murmured a simple thank you, not being up to any bright repartee at that moment. "Just what is going on out there?"

"Some of Jasper's guests earning their keep. Or maybe they're just enjoying themselves. He gathers a queer crew around him."

"It does make a pretty tableau. Is Jasper King one of the knights?"

"No. He's probably watching from somewhere up above."

"You make him sound like a deity."

"He is—within the boundaries of this estate."

I began seeing my new host as a counterpart of my employer, Judson Conroy, a man who needed friends and admirers around him, though on a somewhat different scale.

Jeff said, "Are you feeling better?"

"Much. I'm about back to normal. And you?"

"Fit. How is your appetite?"

"Very much with me."

"Good. I ordered breakfast here in our suite."

"*Our* suite?"

He was amused. "It's larger than you think, pet. That door on the left leads into a common room. It separates the two bedrooms."

"I suppose there's nothing wrong in Jasper King and the others thinking that we are . . ."

"Lovers?" he mocked.

"Yes," I replied coolly. "As long as you don't start believing it yourself."

"Understood." He smiled. "Shall we go to breakfast?"

I accepted the invitation after noting that there had been no damage done by the contesting knights. They now appeared to be toasting each other from a cask that probably contained ale rather than wine. It was a happy, laughing group that surrounded them, and I could only conclude that the mock battle had been a novel pastime in a setting where such odd entertainment was possible.

"They seem to enjoy themselves," I commented as we moved away from the window. "Is Jasper King particularly concerned with the Middle Ages?"

"Not necessarily."

That was all. Jeff went no further, but his troubled frown made me wonder, and when we entered what Jeff had called the common room, Jasper King became even more of an enigma. He no doubt possessed great treasures, but he needed help to put them into some semblance of order and harmony.

The first thing that caught my eye was a John Pimm highboy from the early eighteenth century, graceful but gaudy with its elaborate and confused decorations—japanned panels on the drawer fronts depicting imaginative mythological birds and animals.

Beside it on the tapestried wall was hung a lovely girandole clock, its banjo design topped by an eagle with outspread wings, the banjo end a circular convex mirror that reflected the entire room in miniature.

The two pieces were, of course, mutually accept-able, but nearby was an ornate armchair of Egyptian influence, the terminals of the armrests fashioned into pharaohs' heads. The needlework upholstry carried out the Egyptian motif. The chair was certainly a treasure in itself, but it gave the room the appearance of a museum storage vault. The haphazard pattern of decor was furthered by other pieces, among them a squat, ugly German oak chest upon which sat an exquisite Greek vase with circular artwork showing Athena—I believed—seated before Hercules.

Breakfast was in buffet style, laid out on a veneered piece with rosewood inlay that had once been a French lady's writing desk—and still was, for that matter, regardless of the use it was being now put to.

My impressions were confusing. From the casual use of his art objects—the helter-skelter manner in which they were strewn about—I could only wonder if Jasper King knew their value. The breakfast service was of sterling silver with gleaming English Spode.

Also, there was a touch of necromancy about the breakfast itself. The scrambled eggs were done to per-fection, the rolls in a basket covered by a damask napkin crisp and hot, the coffee piping hot also. But there was not a soul in sight. Whoever delivered it had come and gone.

"Tell me about Jasper King," I said. "When will I meet him?"

Jeff shrugged. "That's hard to say."

"Have you talked to him since we arrived?"

He shook his head.

"Just how well *do* you know Mr. King?"

"That really doesn't matter. What's important is

understanding the man. He's . . . well, he's erratic.''

"People keep saying that, but they don't explain.''

I *was* beginning to understand Jeff. He was a poser, an actor. He possessed a skill at wearing masks. There was his debonair man-of-the-world mask; his pensive, nostalgic pose, wherein he associated himself with a glamorous past and implied a fatalistic attitude concerning the future. These facades were presented, it seemed, with calculated effort toward an impressive image.

His present mood seemed more genuine than any of the others—a frankness that reflected insecurity.

"The thing is, you never know about Jasper. He gave me the Snipe, you know.''

"He *gave* you an expensive airplane? Just like that?''

"One day at Newark airport. He had missed his commercial flight and had to get to Baltimore in a hurry. I flew him down and back, and when we set down at Newark again, he said something about flying in an open cockpit being barbarous and gave me the Snipe.''

My thoughts remained on Jeff more than on the puzzling Jasper King. Jeff had loved the plane. Now it was a wreck somewhere out on the estate. Also, I remembered his conduct during the crash. His bravery, his concern for my safety. That had been genuine, and therein I saw the man to whom I was attracted.

In an added burst of frankness, Jeff said, "There's much hanging in the balance, angel. If this buying expedition works out, I'll be in good shape again.''

"But about Jasper King,'' I said. "If he gave you something as expensive as the Snipe, he must think a great deal of you.''

"Not necessarily. He's the sort of man who can give you a plane today and walk past you tomorrow without saying hello."

"Unstable?"

"You might call him that."

"Then how was he able to amass the fortune he's said to have made?"

"Geniuses can act any way they please and get away with it."

"I suppose so. What about the other guests here at the castle?"

"Hangers-on, freeloaders, sycophants," Jeff said with a shrug calculated to put us in a much higher class.

"If this breakfast is any indication of the service they get, I can hardly blame them for staying around."

"Jasper is stubborn. He clings to his illusions of wealth."

"Jeff, I can't rationalize what I see. A man of that caliber wouldn't hide from the world in a place like this. Egomaniacs do not function as recluses. When did you see Jasper King the last time?"

"In New York some months ago. He was staying at the Plaza and was upset at the way the stock market was acting. We had a few drinks together. He had been trying to borrow money, and he wasn't successful."

"How long has this castle been his headquarters?"

"For well over a year. He sold his estate on Long Island and had everything sent up here."

"Is this your first visit?"

"My second. I was up here for a couple of weeks about six months ago."

"And you were invited up again for this visit?"

"I have a standing invitation," he replied evasively. "I can come whenever I please."

With Jeff in the mood for candor, I continued to question him. I said, "Judson Conroy told me that King's financial troubles are not generally known. But you say he was in New York trying to borrow money. If that's true . . ."

"He was careful about whom he approached."

"Did he approach Judson Conroy?"

"Hardly!"

I pressed on, and the picture clarified. Conroy had gotten his information concerning Jasper King's financial collapse from no other source than Jefferson Stone. Therefore, my presence at the castle was on an even more tenuous basis than I'd imagined. I was in no stronger a position than any other of the partygoers who fawned on King and partook of his largesse.

It had been Jeff's idea that the paintings Judson sought might be available, and with nothing to lose, Conroy had made me his proposition. And Jeff, in desperate need of the commission he'd mentioned, had, up to this moment, furthered the deception in every way possible.

Also, the reason for his sudden honesty was now apparent. We had come to a point where I would learn the truth for myself. Therefore it was better that it should come from him.

I said, "You realize, of course, Jeff, that you're a contemptible person."

His hurt could have been genuine or a gesture of long practice. I could not tell which. "Oh, now, pet. Let's not be too harsh."

"I'm not your pet or your bird or whatever you termed it. That part of the masquerade is over. Please understand that."

"What are you going to do, blow the whole act?"

47

"I'm not quite sure what I'm going to do yet. But tell me—who else here at the castle knows about our fictitious status . . . the romance part?"

"Nobody, yet."

"Then why were we put into this cozy suite together?"

"I guess Callie White assumed it."

"Who is Callie White?"

"A woman. Local. She's lived around here all her life, and she acts as Jasper's hostess. When you fainted out there in the court, she showed up and took over."

"Where can I find her?"

"She's somewhere about."

"Then if you've finished your coffee, I suggest you leave and let me get dressed. Then I'll go find her."

He made no objection. His expression was that of a true gambler who had risked his money on a roll of the dice and lost. The smile with which he rewarded me was patronizing. It said I was a child who did not understand grown-up things and that it was too bad. But what annoyed me most was that it remained so attractive. It brought back flashes of what I'd felt there in his strong arms with the wind and the rain knifing down, and death having just been defeated by an eyelash.

This turned my anger upon myself rather than toward this intruder with the face and body of a lesser god and the heart of a confidence man. If I could not control and direct my emotions, I was no more secure than the other moths who had no doubt circled Jasper King's flame.

However, my resolution was in no way weakened. Perhaps I was in love with Jeff Stone, but that misfortune would not influence me into adopting his precarious way of life.

48

7

She was a tall woman with an arresting face featuring a large, aggressive nose, interesting in that it gave her a Greek profile. A ruler laid along her forehead and the crest of the nose downward would have touched at all points. Her eyes were gray and heavily lashed. She was impressively bosomed, so it was probably her garb that gave her a masculine look—dark trousers encased in half-boots, and a checkered woodsman's shirt open at the throat. Her hair was jet black, drawn back in a bun, and its contrast with the clear gray of her eyes gave them a steely glint. Her manner was pleasant enough.

"You are Karen Spain, I believe. Jeff Stone brought you. I'm Callie White. I see to things for Jasper King."

Perhaps I was being oversensitive, but I didn't like the tone and implication of her greeting—at least, a part of it. The "Jeff-Stone-brought-you" part of it. For I translated that into: You're another of the toys Jasper King's male guests bring along with them.

Before I could reply to her greeting, she went on. "I hope you're feeling better after a night's sleep. I looked in on you once after I got you into bed, and you were doing fine."

"Thank you so much. I'm ashamed, passing out that way."

"You shouldn't be. From what Jeff told me, you did well to hold on as long as you did."

"I think we were both very lucky."

"I'm sure you were. Jeff is marvelous at the stick. A born flier. Losing that plane will break his heart."

I knew what I wanted to say, but now I couldn't find the right words. This put me at a disadvantage, even though Callie White's manner remained friendly.

"Have you and Jeff known each other long?"

"Why do you ask that?"

She laughed. "No particular reason. It's just that from what I've seen around here, Jasper's guests form relationships quickly, and you don't appear to me to be the type."

"As a matter of fact, I hardly know Mr. Stone. He acted as my transportation up here from New York at the behest of Judson Conroy."

"Oh?"

Callie White did not seem particularly interested, but this was confession time, with no room for half-truths.

"I'm here to bid on some of Mr. King's art treasures —that is, if any are for sale."

She made no reply. I could not tell whether this was evasive or again lack of interest. "I think you said you are a local resident—not from the city."

"I was born in Hempstead. I graduated from the University of Illinois because my father went there. Then I came back here to take care of him. I've made quite a study of this location—Caliban's Castle and the estate. I think that's the reason Jasper hired me." She paused to frown. "These people who impose on his hospitality . . ."

She broke off quickly, as though regretting the show of personal dislike. "Would you care to see the castle? It's a fantastic place. I'm sure you'll be amazed."

"I'm already amazed."

Callie fell quickly into the role of tour guide. I sensed her relief as she plunged into a subject obviously dear to her heart.

"Caliban Leach was a twisted genius—a physical horror, if the records can be trusted. But that sad fact may have been instrumental in generating the strength of his mind. Born into English wealth and the British peerage, he was kept hidden from the world by his horrified parents. This no doubt nurtured the bitterness in his soul. Yet, as subsequent events proved, the poor man badly needed love. When he came into his power and his money, he deserted his native land and came west, never to return."

Callie White spoke as from a memorized script, proving her familiarity and interest in her subject. When she paused for breath, I interjected, "That must have been well before the turn of the century."

"It was. He lived temporarily in the South and was probably driven away by the same looks of horror he'd found in England. At any rate, he came to New England and might have gone on into Canada if he had not found this area, a section which was then wild and forbidding but might well have been transplanted bodily from the land he loved. It has the same mixture of topography—dangerous crags, treacherous quicksand stretches, and wide sweeps of moorland sloping toward bluffs overlooking the sea. In season the moors are decked with purple heather—absolutely gorgeous."

While she spoke, I drifted to the window, to find that the two knights were now resting at the table, where the ladies of the court appeared to be fawning on them.

"Caliban no doubt envisioned his castle," Callie said, "but I am of the opinion that Agala was the driving force who brought it into being."

"Agala?"

"Caliban arrived here before the Civil War, and this became a station upon what was called the Underground Railroad along which runaway slaves from the South were moved into Canada. Agala was a Haitian beauty—of royal blood herself, I suspect. While her background could not be traced accurately, I think she killed a planter in Georgia who demanded the privileges of ownership. Agala would have been desired by any man who looked upon her. At any rate, she fled with a band of escaped slaves and got this far north. Here she stayed, and in Agala, Caliban Leach found the love he so badly needed.''

Not quite the romantic Callie seemed to be, I could only wonder whether it had been love or opportunism that motivated Agala, but I said nothing.

"They had a child, a daughter, as beautiful as her mother, I'm sure. But little is known of her. Perhaps she went back to England after her parents' tragic end.''

"Tragic?"

"Yes. Caliban died, his poor distorted body putting him to torture there at the end. He passed on in Agala's arms, and she followed him soon afterward—a suicide, I'm sure. They are buried side-by-side out on the moor that Caliban Leach loved so dearly.''

In spite of myself, I was caught up in the romantic aspects of the tragedy, even though I suspected that time and Callie White had probably fictionalized it somewhat.

"What happened to the castle after Caliban's death?" I asked.

"The wealth he left behind was claimed by relatives in England. There were legal complications, but they won the bulk of it.''

"How old was the daughter at that time?"

"She was of age, and as I said, probably went back

to England. Caliban and Agala died in the late eighteen-nineties, and while I did a great deal of research on Caliban Leach, the expense in money and time became too great. You see, I planned to do a book on the man and the Leach dynasty, but I never got around to it. Perhaps someday I will.''

"I hope you do. It would be a fantastic story."

"In order to complete it satisfactorily I would have to go to England and research the villain of the piece, Neville Leach. He was the descendant who came to America and took all Caliban's wealth back to England.''

I wondered why Callie classed the man as a villain. If he had legal rights, the pursuit of Caliban Leach's fortune seemed honorable.

There was a knock at the door at that moment, and Callie went to answer it. She spoke to someone beyond my range of vision, then said to me, "I'm sorry I can't show you around. Jasper is calling for me. But please feel free to explore by yourself, and we'll meet later.''

I now regretted the historical trend our conversation had taken. I would have much preferred a discussion as to my chances of facing Jasper King on a straightforward basis with an honest presentation of my reason for being there.

Callie paused at the door. "Just two warnings," she said. "You'd best not go down into the caves alone. That would be dangerous. Also, don't wander too far from the castle. We have a marauder. A brown bear has wandered down out of the woods to the north. It killed a man the other night.''

With that, she was gone, and I would of course take heed of her warnings. I could not recall having heard about the caves she mentioned, but they sounded ominous. And I certainly had no intention of challenging a hostile bear on its own ground. However, I looked forward to exploring the castle. After my traumatic introduction to the place in the dead of night, it would be like meeting a monster made less terrifying by the light of a bright sun.

8

My first encounter was with a replica of ancient times. A knight in armor.

I'd turned to the right from the door to my quarters and moved along a narrow stone walkway open to the central square through arched vents in even series that ran around three sides of the great castle, this plan of architecture duplicated also on the third level above me.

I turned the southeast corner of the castle and came upon a stairway that took me down into a sort of foyer, although proportionately larger than most rooms into which a foyer would lead.

A shining suit of armor confronted me, misplaced in that it was in the center of the floor rather than against a wall, where most such artifacts are placed. As I entered, it turned in forlorn confusion and said, "Will someone help me out of this sardine can?"

I approached and lifted the pointed visor in the helmet. A pair of angry brown eyes in a not unhandsome young face glared out at me.

"They deserted me because I didn't win," he complained. "But I did fight to a draw. That should get me some consideration, don't you think?"

"I'm sure it should," I replied. "How did you get into the suit in the first place?"

"Oh, they were all there to help. I guess they were disappointed because neither of us drew blood."

"We'll try to get the helmet off first," I said, and

searched for the stays that held it in place. I loosened them and lifted.

"Ouch! Watch it, for heaven's sake! You're taking my ears off!"

"Sorry. You should have pinned your ears back before you put it on."

The helmet came free, and I was looking at a finely chiseled face under tousled curly brown hair, more the face of an artist than of a warrior.

"Thanks," the young man said. He squinted at me as he played gingerly with his right ear. "I'm Rory Talbott. I haven't seen you around. Who are you?"

I told him, and asked, "What comes next? The breastplate?"

"I guess so. It ties behind."

Leather thongs held it in place. I undid them, and half the job seemed completed. Rory Talbott took a deep breath. "Thanks," he said.

Then an inner door opened, and a girl appeared. I could not clearly identify her but assumed she was one of the ladies of the court who had changed from the lovely gown of King Arthur's time into a rather daring shift that stopped at mid-knee.

One thing *was* clear. She resented me. An angry look proved this, as she turned just as angrily on the half-stripped knight.

"Why did you stop here?" she demanded. "Why didn't you come with us?"

"Why did the rest of you rush off and leave me with a stuck visor?"

"Oh, you're just too helpless for words. Come along with me."

More mindful of his manners, Rory Talbott said,

"This is Karen Spain, an angel of mercy. Karen, meet Ginger Wade. She rushes off and leaves people to their doom."

The girl acknowledged the introduction with a surly nod and pulled at Rory Talbott's arm.

"Come along. If I don't watch you every minute . . ."

The rest of it was cut off by the slamming of the door through which she had appeared and now dragged the discomfited knight after her.

I chose not to follow, turning rather in the opposite direction to search out the flashes of color I'd seen through the narrow openings along the upper corridor. I passed through the outer doorway and gasped.

The loveliness I beheld was almost beyond belief. But more startling because a tropical glory such as this did not belong under the open sky of temperate New England.

The jungle—no other term was appropriate—had apparently been left to itself. Without benefit of a gardener's attentions, it seemed to have mystically disciplined itself to the proportions afforded it—a square section of the inner courtyard of the castle, which stretched some hundred yards or so. The slipper orchids that blazed out at me in purple grandeur were rooted in the trunk of a jacaranda tree, itself aglow with its own bluish-purple blossoms. Nearby, in friendly entanglement, were the fragile white and yellow flowers of the frangipani. A small Judas tree, not in bloom, appeared to be tending the flaming blossoms of a royal poinciana, the latter nowhere near its accustomed majestic height but otherwise of regal health.

Centrally located, a squat magnolia with its own

57

foot-long pink blossoms appeared to be playing gracious host to floral beauties from lands of tropical climate belting the earth.

But even in all the beauty confronting me, there were suggestions of menace. Squatting near the trunk of a stunted, splay-topped sego palm was a sinister curare, the source of dreaded South American poison for the tips of lethal arrows and blowgun ammunition. With little room to thrive, it was more a strong-limbed bush than the ancestral tree form of its native land, but still easily identifiable.

As I moved closer, my first surge of pleasure faded. Perhaps a cloud passing over the sun at that exact moment had something to do with it, but I suffered a sudden chill, emotional rather than physical, because in the humid, tropical heat coming up from somewhere below, a physical chill was impossible.

I questioned the feeling, and while the cause remained obscure, it seemed to shape up as a resentment. None of this belonged. Someone in the past had gathered these lovely strangers together and forced them to live where they did not belong. They survived and prospered, I was sure, in defiance rather than gratitude.

There was something else, something missing, that troubled me. Then I realized what it was. The silence. There were no birds to add their joy and color to this miniature tropical setting. Only a faint, steady, persistent hissing sound, as though a congress of asps and vipers waited below, communing with each other and biding their time. The faint sound came, of course, from the thermal fault, which had been revealed to me so spectacularly on the previous night, that natural furnace which made Caliban Leach's creation unique among castles.

The cloud passed over, but my spirits lifted only moderately. I moved on, skirting the jungle. A Strelitzia, the incredible bird-of-paradise flower with the flared orange coxcomb, thrust its blue tongue out at me, and I expected to hear a raucous challenge to my presence there. But only silence.

Caliban's Castle, it seemed, was a place where beauty and menace, grandeur and formless threat, went hand-in-hand.

I rounded the jungle and found less unbelievable aspects, if one could accept the basic medieval environment itself. The rest of the open courtyard was done in flagstone, with a circular fountain in the center. The south corner abutting the gate wall, from which the drawbridge protruded, was evidently a stable. The wagon in which we had been brought from the cottage stood by, and there was the impatient neigh of a horse from within.

No one was in sight, the square deserted there under the hot sun. Its unclouded blaze plus the heat coming up from below made the place uncomfortably hot. I approached the fountain, in which water bubbled up in a single jet, to fall into a circular pool. The water looked inviting, but that was an illusion. When I dipped my hand in, I found it warm and limpid.

A stone bench circled the fountain. I sat down and tried to turn my mind away from my surroundings and onto my personal problems. Callie White had assured me that we would meet again. I was certain that we would, but to what purpose? Still, she was the only contact I had with Jasper King, discounting Jeff Stone, whom I felt to be in my debit column rather than an asset. A reference to be avoided at any audience with Jasper King.

Yet it was Jeff who remained foremost in my mind, the one I needed most.

Then, as though the mere wish were enough to gain an answer, I heard a cry of excitement from above. I looked upward, and my heart stopped.

On the edge of the parapet high above, his arms spread like the wings of an uncertain bird, I saw Jeff Stone walking the edge of the parapet, where a single misstep would send him hurtling down to his death on the flagstones below. . . .

9

I could neither move nor speak. I could only watch, frozen, fearful that the smallest whisper on my part would bring him down to final disaster.

My mind was in chaos as I asked what madness had overtaken him. Was he drunk? Had depression at the loss of his plane driven him to this insane form of suicide?

From somewhere up there beyond range of my vision, he was being encouraged, but tones in the voices reflected excitement rather than alarm—the same level of intense pleasure I'd heard during the knightly duel on the lawn.

As I watched, Jeff stopped, wavered precariously, then moved on. I tried to discern the goal of his mad walk on the castle parapet and decided it was the wall of the watchtower at the southwest juncture. That left him some twenty-five feet to go.

He progressed step by uncertain step, and I realized he was not drunk or he would have fallen long since. I found myself praying silently in my mind. Oh, dear Lord, help him. Allow him to live. Even as I did so, I told myself that my horror was no greater than if I had been watching a complete stranger up there risking his life. But that was merely a feeble attempt to deny far deeper emotion. Love? I still refused the term, even as the possibility of the next few moments sickened me.

With a final rushing step, Jeff reached his goal. He leaned against the circular wall of the watchtower, and I sensed his sigh of relief. A cheer went up from the invisible watchers above. Then Jeff stepped down to the safety of the parapet walk and disappeared from my view.

I sat there on the fountain bench, weak from the traumatic shock. And quite naturally, with the danger past, a surge of anger replaced my fright. Why should I worry about an idiot so unstable as to play madmen's games such as I had just witnessed? Anyone fool enough to love such a person deserved all the misery that such a love would bring. I tried to replace Jeff's image in my mind with that of steady, sane, sensible Max Bowman. That brought guilt as I realized that I had given Max scarcely a thought since boarding Jeff Stone's plane at Newark airport for a trip to heaven-knew-where. Max was the one who should have been in my heart and my mind while facing death in that storm. I should have been yearning for his arms and his protection while Jeff carried me away from the wreck; that, instead of finding wanton excitement in the arms of a comparative stranger.

All of which highlighted a grim fact. It was my own stability that was in question, not that of an attractive neurotic who fed on dreams and illusions.

Even as I harshly assessed my shortcomings, I had left the fountain and was climbing a flight of stairs in the south wall toward the section upon which Jeff had walked. My excuse was fallacious, but it was all I had—to see for myself what sort of people would encourage another to such stupid reaches of folly.

I did not reach the upper level, which was probably just as well. Callie White came striding along the corridor on the second level. She called to me, "Karen, I've been hunting for you."

I waited, and as she approached, a look of concern dawned. "What on earth! You're white as flour. Did you see a ghost?"

"Hardly that," I replied. "I just saw an idiot try to kill himself."

She listened to my account of what had happened without any great reaction. When I finished, she shrugged. "They're a hollow bunch, all of them."

"Who are they? *What* are they? I met one of them this morning and helped pry him out of a suit of armor."

"You'll better understand their philosophy when you realize they haven't any. They make up a younger generation who use the depression as an excuse to do nothing. They live from day to day and help no one, least of all themselves."

"But the desperate games they play . . ."

"I think they try to convince themselves they have courage, while they're really cowards running away from life."

"Why does Jasper King tolerate them? From what I've heard of him, he's quite the opposite—a man with ambition, who made millions."

Callie White was basically a positive person. I'd first seen her as having masculine traits. Now that impression had changed. Callie was aggressively feminine; far different. A handsome woman by any standards, she would be attractive to men who had an affinity with strength.

A positive person, but again, there was that uncertainty when Jasper King's name came up. The troubled frown, the hesitation.

Finally she said, "Jasper has compassion. His guests

are mainly the children of vanished wealth, you might say, and some of them *have* seen tragedy. Young Talbott, for instance . . ."

"I met him. He was the one in the suit of armor."

"Rory is one of the Long Island Talbotts. His sole training is in useless liberal arts and skill on the polo field. His father was a millionaire one day and a pauper the next—wiped out on Wall Street. He jumped from his office window, some twenty floors up. His mother went off on someone's yacht."

"How tragic."

"I'm sure," Callie replied indifferently. "But why I called you—I relayed our conversation to Jasper, and he wants to see you."

"To order me off the premises, no doubt."

The observation did not sit well with Callie. I got the impression from her quick look that she did not care for whiners, and I was sorry I'd sounded like one.

"You never can tell," she replied. "But I promise you won't be shot at sunrise."

My nervousness was quite overshadowed by my curiosity as we approached Jasper King's suite. It was on the top level of the castle in the northeast corner, properly secluded, as would befit the lord of the manor. And as often happens in such cases, what I found inside was about the last thing I expected. Spartan simplicity instead of the opulent luxury I had visualized. No priceless works of art on the walls. A cot, a chair, and a plain pine table strewn with papers; this in stark contrast to the expensive pieces scattered carelessly about in my own rooms.

I was not surprised at Jasper King's personal appearance, because I'd formed no mental picture of him. I found a tall, thin, dark man who looked to be a dynamically preserved sixtyish, who exuded an aura of somber power. I was sure I sensed that power, but still I questioned myself. Was it actually there, or was it only in my mind as something to be expected because of his reputation? I could only wonder if I would be around long enough to find out.

His eyes held to me unwaveringly, with no variance of expression, while Callie introduced me. When he spoke, his voice was soft and throaty.

"Calpurnia tells me you came here to bid on paintings," he said.

I did not miss Callie White's reaction to his use of the name she obviously hated. Then she left the room, and Jasper King and I were alone.

"That's true, Mr. King. But to be perfectly honest, you may find good reason to reject me."

"Honesty," he mused. "It's either your virtue or a device you use. I wonder which."

"If you feel it is the latter, there is no point in further discussion, is there? I'd better leave and take up no more of your time."

"Please sit down."

I did so because it was more of an invitation than a command and I could maintain my dignity by telling myself I was not obeying an order. Jasper King sat down on the edge of the cot and continued to regard me thoughtfully.

"You are here, I understand, on a commission from Judson Conroy, rather deviously, that is."

"Perhaps Callie White did not tell you why. It was because Mr. Conroy felt you would not deal with him directly."

"And you do not consider it disloyal to your employer, telling me this?"

"It was a matter of circumstance. I feel that I was deceived and used by Mr. Conroy. Therefore, any loyalty to him was canceled out by his tactics."

"I see. But if given the opportunity to bid on my artworks, you would still do so to his benefit?"

"Yes. As long as you have been made aware of the truth in the matter. However, with hard feeling between you and Mr. Conroy, I doubt if I'll be given the opportunity."

He smiled for the first time, a mixture of quiet amusement and a seeming touch of sadness. He said, "We often construct our own obstacles and place them in our own paths. Conroy has a talent for such things. He is stupid to imagine that I would let a personal dislike interfere with a business matter."

"That was my own reaction when he told me you two were not on a friendly basis."

The smiled flashed again, then faded. "Frankly, I think there is more to Conroy's intrigue than a few paintings."

"Are you saying he is really not interested in buying art?"

"Oh, I'm sure he is. But he is probably in contact with others who want to find out if my art collection is really for sale."

"I'm afraid I don't understand."

"The financial world has many angles. It is a great advantage to know a man's true situation. This can be done in many ways. For instance, if a man in my position is forced to sell his art collection, it could indicate weakness in other areas where predators are waiting to pounce on him. Just as wolves wait for signs of weakness in a deer or an elk, the wolves of finance look for the same signs in those they prey upon."

"Then you are saying that Judson Conroy would be interested in knowing if your collection is for sale even if I were not permitted to bid."

"I suspect as much."

"Mr. King . . . I don't know what to say. I'm confused."

"Then perhaps I'd better tell you my reason for calling you here."

"I would be grateful."

"In one respect, I have great faith in Conroy's ability. He knows art, and he knows the individual. So whoever he would send up here would have to be an expert. And I have work for an expert."

"If there is anything . . ."

"There is. I would like you to appraise and catalog my collection. As long as you have canceled yourself out on Conroy's commission, perhaps you would work for me in that capacity."

I came close to jumping at his offer. To study firsthand the treasures in Jasper King's collection! To examine and pore over Gauguins, Corots, Van Goghs, and perhaps even some examples of the old Italian masters! The opportunity dazzled me.

But my common sense prevailed. Overeagerness could only diminish me in Jasper King's regard.

I asked, "Exactly what do you have in mind? *Are* you planning to put your collection on the market?"

"In these difficult times, planning ahead is difficult. The collection was delivered here from several different locations. An inventory is in order, no matter what develops in the future."

"As I said, my qualifications—"

"We've gone over that," he replied impatiently. "I'd like your decision."

"Could I have a little time to consider it? Perhaps a few hours? All this is so abrupt."

"Of course. Please come back when you have made your decision."

"Thank you. . . ."

I left his apartment with the feeling that I'd been *too* reluctant. I was giving him an opportunity to change his mind, and he was known to be eccentric.

I was tempted to knock on his door and give him my answer immediately. I resisted, and went to find Jeff Stone. . . .

10

Quickly locating any single individual in an establishment as large as Caliban's Castle could be a problem. I found it so.

The square was deserted upon my return, not strange in light of the tropical temperature. No doubt Jasper King's guests had sought cooler places. I would probably have gone on searching if I had not been sidetracked when I opened a likely-looking door on the second level and was rewarded for my intrusion by finding a library.

From its appearance, Jasper King also needed a librarian. While some books had been placed on the shelves, far more were strewn about the floor in stacks, with others still in their crates. My first reaction was one of dismay. If there were any rare volumes in the collection, they were being shabbily treated.

I began browsing and found at least one—a beautiful Bible in Latin, tooled in red leather and lovingly illuminated in a manner that suggested monks of the Middle Ages who were faithful to God and to the preservation of enlightenment, so easily destroyed by vandalism and savagery.

Placing the book carefully upon a shelf, I searched further, and perhaps because I was subconsciously interested in the subject, a book entitled *Castles of Britain* caught my eye. I thumbed through it and was quickly convinced that it would tell me about the castle, and perhaps, through implication, something of Caliban Leach himself.

I took the book with me, and on the way back to my quarters, I again came upon Callie White. She tried to make the meeting appear casual, but I got the impression that she had been hovering about waiting for me. She hurried toward me. "Oh, Jasper has finished with you."

Then, before I could frame a reply, she saw my book. Her gray-blue eyes lightened. "You are interested in architecture?"

"Well, not exactly. But I found this book on castles, so I borrowed it."

"I promised to show you about, so let's get to it. I suggest we go up into a watchtower so that you can get a bird's-eye view of the whole establishment."

Her enthusiasm would have been difficult to deny even if I'd been so inclined. She led me briskly up staircases and along corridors, and finally up a stifling walkway into the southeast watchtower.

The trip was worth it. From that vantage point the whole of Caliban Leach's estate was laid out in panorama; some five hundred acres, Callie told me.

She said, "The castle is planned on the lines of Beaumaris, one of the classic Gothics in England, but Caliban Leach had ideas of his own. Beaumaris has both a north and a south gatehouse. Caliban built in a single entrance, as you can see. Also, he eliminated the middle towers, erecting them only at the four corners of the castle."

As Callie's technical treatise went on, I found my mind wandering to the broader aspects of the scene below me. I said, "You mentioned that Caliban Leach and Agala are buried together somewhere on the estate."

"Yes." She turned and pointed across the waving

purple expanse of heather that sloped toward the sea. "Just there," she said. "That promontory at the bluff line. A sentimental choice, I imagine. From there Caliban could look in both directions—back across the sea toward the land he loved, from which he had exiled himself, and in this direction over the makeshift England he created out of his loneliness."

I thought that quite poetic, but it appeared to be accidental so far as the practical-minded Callie White was concerned. I peered toward the spot she indicated and said, "I see that the graves are kept up."

That surprised her. "Hardly. As a matter of fact, the exact location is not known for sure."

"But someone appears to be tending them."

We now squinted across the distance together. Callie frowned. "That figure. I wish we'd brought a glass."

As it was, we could make out only the figure itself, human definitely.

"Kneeling?" Callie asked.

"I think so. He or she appears to be digging— weeding around the graves, or perhaps planting flowers."

"Curious," Callie replied. "I know of no one who could be remotely interested."

With no immediate answer, she lost interest. She turned her gaze downward and said, "That moat should be drained. It's a stagnant pesthole. I don't know how it could be done, though."

"Where does the water come from?"

"It seeps up from below, just enough to offset evaporation on the surface."

"Does Jasper King own the estate?"

"Yes. On a staggering mortgage."

"He plans to sell?"

It did not seem to occur to Callie that she might be giving confidential information to a comparative stranger. "Sell?" she said. "Lose it, I'm afraid. Jasper is terribly worried. He has retreated to this last stronghold and seems to be standing the world off behind these thick walls."

"There are rumors that he is in financial trouble."

"I think they are well-founded. Every day he goes up into his watchtower—over there on the northeast corner—and broods. The tower is locked off. No one is allowed there."

"I suppose when a man suddenly loses millions . . ."

"Yes. And the death of his wife . . ."

That new revelation struck me sharply. "What wife?"

Callie seemed surprised. "You didn't know?"

A few moments' thought, and I realized that that was not too strange. Those who had directed my course toward Jasper King were not sentimentally oriented. Judson Conroy could not have cared less about Jasper King's tragic aspects, other than with the hope that they had softened him up for the kill. And Jeff Stone, trying only to survive, would just not have bothered to mention any of Jasper King's losses other than his money.

"When did it happen?"

"Shortly before Jasper came up here from Long Island. I saw his wife but once, sometime earlier than that—when they were searching for a secluded location and I showed them the castle. She was younger than Jasper, some ten years, I'd say. Strikingly attractive. In fact, you reminded me of her strongly. You have the same erect bearing, the same coloring."

"I take that as a compliment."

Callie ignored that with a frown. "They came and I

72

showed them the castle, and then they left. Later I heard of the tragedy and thought it probably ended all chance of making the deal.''

''You were involved in selling the castle to Jasper King?''

''Yes. It was owned by a California syndicate. I acted as their agent.''

Little by little, for whatever the worth, I was getting a more complete picture. Callie went on.

''But Jasper did come back. He bought Caliban's Castle and moved in. The California people were happy to get rid of it. They took the mortgage themselves.''

Poor Jasper! No one had time to drop a tear for his sorrow. They were all too busy trying to profit from his misfortunes. Still, I could not blame them too greatly. I myself was there for the same purpose, comparing the personal advantages of the two offers—Jasper King's or that of Judson Conroy.

''By the way,'' Callie said, suddenly remembering. ''What did he want of you?''

''To straighten out his inventory. He wants his art-works cataloged and organized.''

''Getting ready to sell, I suppose. Do you feel up to a job like that?''

''I can only try.''

''You'll find him generous enough. He isn't niggardly in paying for services.''

I was getting used to hearing all things measured in terms of money, so I was not bothered by Callie's pecuniary attitude.

''We didn't discuss money. I haven't given him my final answer.''

''I'd take the job, if I were you. What can you lose?''

Callie's cordial reaction eased my mind. She did not

seem to feel that her own position would be threatened if I accepted Jasper King's proposition. Evidently there would be no palace-guard rivalry between us.

"I'd be grateful for any help you could give me," I said.

"I'm afraid that wouldn't be much. I know very little about art."

"I was referring to the castle. You know it from top to bottom, and Jasper King's treasures seem to be spread all over the place."

"I suppose that's true. The thing for you to do is go through the castle room by room. I can give you a couple of helpers if you want anything moved."

"I'd appreciate that."

"I must go now. Anytime you want me, you had best look in the kitchen. It's to the right as you enter the great hall behind the garden. In the basement. Jasper expects efficiency and good service, so I make my headquarters down there close to the staff."

"Thank you. And please don't let me keep you."

She hurried off, and I felt that I had made some gains. In the preceding hour I had been given the run of the castle by both Jasper King *and* his housekeeper. My anger at Jeff Stone's insane prank had cooled somewhat, so I postponed confronting him and again turned my attention across the purple moor where I'd seen the figure crouching over the graves of Caliban Leach and Agala. It was a considerable walk from the castle, but the day was nice, all signs of the storm having passed. So I surrendered to an urge for a closer look.

Seen from across the drawbridge and toward the sea bluffs, the sinister aspects of Caliban's Castle dissipated to a great extent. Still, not completely so. As I walked through the field of waving heather, the beauty of it was clouded by an aura of bleak loneliness, a depressing factor difficult to put into words. I fell into what might have been termed a *Wuthering Heights* mood, a mental attitude ripe for fantasy. I turned to gaze at the rugged crags to the northwest of the castle and visualized Heathcliff waiting impatiently for his Cathy; then the star-crossed girl herself hurrying to the arms of the lover she could not resist. And I wondered if Caliban Leach, a figure fully as tragic, had walked these moors and yearned for his native land.

But enough of that, I told myself, and went briskly on until I came to the location there on the bluff which Callie had pointed out as Caliban Leach's resting place.

It was now deserted, the figure I'd seen having vanished. There were indeed two graves, unmarked save for the rectangular indications there in the earth. And they had been lately tended. Time and weather had hollowed the surfaces, but now fresh earth had been used to mound them over and restore the fresh appearance. They were now bordered in newly planted greenery.

This raised an intriguing question. Who was responsible for this sentimental gesture? Only Callie White, to my knowledge, even knew the location of the graves. And none of the others I had met would have bothered to find out, let alone indulge in any mark of respect.

I walked on to the edge of the nearby bluff and looked down at the sea. A narrow, rock-strewn beach bordered the ocean in both directions. Also, there was a path of sorts down to the shore, a precarious descent cut into the wall of the bluff, off which one could tumble with a single misstep. The earth was soft at that point, soft enough to hold footprints, and those I discovered brought a quick, unbidden chill. They came from the direction of the graves and went down the narrow pathway. Someone had escaped by that route. But the eerie part was the emptiness and silence below. The long stretch of beach in both directions was utterly deserted. Nor were any of the rocks there below large enough to hide a human being.

On the basis of what I could see, my mysterious grave tender had gone down the path and walked off into the sea.

Not likely, I told myself firmly, in an effort to shake off my sudden fear. Fright was a totally unjustified reaction. Nothing in that open, deserted place could possibly harm me.

A child could have been understandably frightened under such circumstances, but I was an adult. Thus I was ashamed of my childish timidity and sought to justify it logically in order to salve my ego. I found the justification by remembering the bear against which I had been warned.

Of course! I'd foolishly wandered too far from the castle. What if the beast was crouching in one of the thick clusters that dotted my path back to the castle? I would have to face that danger, and I built upon it, thus replacing a childish fear with a more realistic one as I returned to the castle.

Upon my closer approach, there was another disquieting incident. My route led me toward the northeast corner of the castle, and when I glanced upward, I saw a figure standing on the watchtower there. It was the locked-off tower over Jasper King's quarters, and as I came nearer, I could see that it was King himself posed there against the blue sky, a part of the silhouette of the great structure.

Obviously the tower had a flat roof with a foot-high balustrade running around it, because King was visible from the ankles up. He was hardly a heroic figure as he stood there without movement. His head was bent as though in mourning or deep contemplation. His hands were clasped behind his back, and though I felt that his eyes were upon me in a steady gaze, he made no gesture, no motion.

The unwavering stare I suspected made me uneasy even at that distance. I raised my hand and waved to him. He did not respond, and somehow—perhaps from growing inner tension I did not myself realize—I sensed an entirely different person than the one who had interviewed me and offered me the tempting assignment.

I recalled the reactions of both Callie White and Jeff Stone during the conversations concerning Jasper King, their looks of troubled uncertainty. In both cases I had assumed that they knew something about the obscure tycoon they did not see fit to tell me. Now that opinion was somewhat altered. The three of us might well be in the same boat, seeking answers to questions that confused all three of us.

At any rate, I told myself, in a comparatively short time I had been put into a more favorable position to find those answers.

I reached the moat and began circling it toward the drawbridge, Jasper King—in my mind—grotesquely one with the gargoyles that grimaced rigidly along the upper rim of Caliban's Castle. . . .

11

"All right," Jeff retorted. "What do you want me to do? Show the white feather to those clowns? Do you want them to think I've lost my nerve?"

"You might show them a little character. If they dared you to jump from the roof into the moat, would you do it?"

"Don't be ridiculous!"

"Really! Is what you did up there on the parapet any less ridiculous?"

He smiled through the candlelight at our table. "You didn't see all of it. After I made it, Rory Talbott backed down. He wouldn't take the chance."

"Talbott. He was one of the two in the armor fighting out on the lawn."

"The other one was Ken Latham. They'll be a little more careful with their challenges after this."

We were in the great dining hall of the castle. A magnificent walnut dining table of banquet length dominated the center behind which a walk-in fireplace faithfully duplicated the cooking and heating facilities of the ancient English models. The fireplace was of no practical value, what with the thermal fault heating the room and the more modern kitchen in the basement, but the image had been faithfully preserved.

Some other changes had been made. Perhaps in order to soften the medieval harshness of the hall, smaller tables had been placed to one side for more intimate dining, with Jasper King's obvious penchant for luxury still prevailing. Rich damask tablecloths and napkins.

Sterling silver and gleaming china. This display, along with other manifestations of wealth, indicated that if Jasper King was going down the financial drain, he planned to do it with all flags flying.

"Jeff, why do you find it necessary to impress those people? Who are they, exactly?"

He avoided my first question by answering the second. "A Long Island crowd. Snobs, all of them. Their parents fawned on Jasper King, and not one of them is equipped to make a living in difficult times. Maybe Jasper feels responsible for them, I don't know. Anyhow, they're up here waiting out the depression."

"And trying to kill each other?"

"It's a form of defiance, I think. Their way of staving off boredom."

"Jasper King's reason for tolerating them is academic, Jeff. What bothers me is your letting them victimize you. That mad risk . . ."

"Maybe I'm bored also. But why should it bother you? Why should you care one way or another?"

I had no ready reply. I refused to concede that I'd fallen in love with Jeff Stone. Yet there seemed no other reason for my concern.

I replied evasively. "After all, you did save my life."

"And my own along with it. Let's get out of here. The place is depressing."

The dinner had been buffet style, excellent in every detail, the coffee especially. As we left the dining hall, I commented on the gourmet aspects of Jasper King's hospitality. Jeff shrugged. "It wasn't bad," he said, and I thought I understood. Jeff, possibly more so than the others, was a professional guest, an attractive person welcomed in the best circles, and therefore the best was commonplace to him. Perhaps, I thought, that accounted for his restlessness. What with the depression, he was running out of wealthy hosts.

I also rationalized other aspects of Jeff Stone. In the beginning, his attentions to me had been romantic pursuit. He had brought all his charm to bear, but as a personal reassurance rather than from any great interest in me. Jeff had to keep proving himself lest his glamour fade. He saw my interest in him as a form of surrender. This was enough to satisfy him.

I was saddened rather than disappointed, and perhaps irritated at seeing his obvious potential going to waste. However, I had more important things to think about. I certainly had no intention of taking on the added responsibility of retracking Jeff Stone's life.

That declaration brought me up short. Perhaps it explained a great deal about me as a person—why, at twenty-five, I was still unattached, a fairly attractive female without a love in my life, without a man plotted into my future. I was too prone to find flaws in the male sex. This repelled possible suitors and sent them searching elsewhere. All except Max, of course, but at the moment he seemed far away, part of another life. Thus had this new environment, Caliban's Castle and this strange assortment of people, placed a subtle hold on me.

Out in the open square with the perfume of flowers around us and a yellow moon overhead, Jeff and I still found nothing to talk about. He excused himself and hurried away, and I sat by the fountain alone, reconciling myself—after a fashion—to my fate. Karen Spain was the independent woman, incapable of accepting a man on the blind terms of love for its own sake.

How wrong I was!

12

There was a modern intercom system throughout the castle, and my bedside phone jangled me awake in the dead of night. After struggling back to consciousness I snapped on the light and looked at my watch.

Three A.M.

I picked up the phone. It was Jasper King. "Miss Spain, will you be so good as to come to my quarters?"

Sensing a crisis, a disaster of some sort, I did not question the invitation or the command—whichever— and replied, "Right away."

I was ready in scant minutes and slipped out into the silent walkway around the inner perimeter of the castle, intent upon hurrying to the northeast corner.

But there was an interlude as the night spell of Caliban's Castle reached out to hold me. There below, with the sunless air chilling the jungle, a haze drifted lazily upward, the seeming frosty breath of a monster waiting in the caves under the square.

The caves. It was an area of the castle unfamiliar to me. Callie White had warned me against going down there. But I was not a child, and I resolved to do a little exploring as soon as my time permitted.

Meanwhile, the castle continued to exert its spell. A fanciful impression that the brooding spirit of Caliban Leach remained here rather than out on the moor in his newly tended grave; a sense of tangible mind-stuff plotting the destinies of mere humans who tried feebly to control their own fate.

I shuddered and hurried on, up to the third level and

to Jasper King's door. I knocked. There was no response. A second knock brought the same result. I waited for a time, then gathered my courage and opened the door.

The lights were on, and beyond the foyer I saw the Spartan quarters which had surprised me on my previous visit. I called out, "Mr. King, it's Karen Spain. . . ."

No reply. I went through the foyer and into the main room. Doors giving off in two directions indicated the suite as being laid out in the same manner as my own—a common room, with bedrooms at either end. But here the windowed wall was foreshortened, and another door, slightly ajar, occupied that space. It had to lead to the watchtower upon which I had seen Jasper King standing when I'd returned from the sea bluffs. Perhaps he was again keeping his vigil with loneliness. Still, he *had* summoned me, so I felt justified in making my presence known.

I approached the door, then paused. He was speaking to someone up there, and I decided to wait and not intrude. His voice came to me, low but still quite clear. As I listened, I felt some guilt as an eavesdropper, then forgot that aspect completely as the words came down to me.

"Shall I compare thee to a summer's day?
Thou art more lovely and more temperate.
Rough winds do shake the darling buds of May,
And summer's lease hath all too short a date . . ."

I heard the immortal verse out to the end, recognizing it as one of Shakespeare's most romantic sonnets.

As I did so, my opinion of Jasper King changed sharply. I'd seen him, from previous descriptions, as being a keen industrialist and financier not given to romanticism. After meeting him, I'd tempered that a little—a man facing defeat, wearied by the battle, confused by the defeats he had suffered.

Now, a new insight into the lord of the castle. A man deeply in love.

As a new devotion began—"How do I love thee? Let me count the ways . . ."—I drew back from my eavesdropping. But not until there in the half-light I'd gotten a fair idea of what lay beyond the mysterious door. It led into a circular anteroom running to the size of the tower itself. A flight of stone steps led downward on one side, and a spiral iron staircase wound upward into the tower itself through the anteroom ceiling—to where Jasper King's tender rendezvous was taking place.

I fled. No other term would better describe my flight from the place as the shame of my intrusion literally took me by the throat. Shame sent me rushing back to my own quarters; and for a reason I could not understand, I was completely undone—trembling, shaken, far beyond any point the experience should have justified. I was tempted to knock on the door of Jeff Stone's bedroom and seek the comfort of his presence. Personal pride blocked the impulse, and I finally crawled into bed, where I huddled, miserable and confused.

It was only then that I realized I was chilled to the bone, also a new experience. I had never before realized that fright could congeal the blood in that manner. There was a sense of Jasper King's quarters having been very cold. That, of course, was not possible, what with the thermal fault heating the entire castle to tropical warmth.

Eventually I drifted off into restless sleep, my subconscious mind remaining alert to dangers it suspected, even if my upper consciousness had no way of interpreting them.

I awoke to bright sunlight coming in through the high windows of my bedroom. It was late. Evidently I'd fallen into sound sleep and no one had disturbed me.

There *had* been a visit. I realized this when I saw the breakfast laid out on the French writing desk. Again the skill of Jasper King's seemingly invisible staff—trained to serve but not to disturb.

The breakfast had long since turned cold. Fortunately I had no appetite, and the orange juice was my only need.

As I bathed and dressed, I pondered my adventure of the previous night. Now, in the clear light of day, it had all the consistency of a dream, so much so that I had to ask myself if I'd really been called by Jasper King. Had I really left my bed in answer to his summons?

My doubts vanished when I realized I might now be in his bad graces by having failed to await his pleasure. My quick uneasiness at that thought proved, if nothing else, that my desire to accept his offer was far stronger than I realized. Otherwise his treatment of me would certainly have been annoying.

I decided not to await developments and went to the intercom, where I pushed the button opposite ''Northeast Tower'' on the directory board. As I waited, I shaped my white lie.

When he answered, his voice had lost the emotional

cadences I'd heard the previous night. It was crisp and businesslike.

"Mr. King. I'm sorry about last night. I did go to your quarters in answer to your call."

"My call?"

"Around three o'clock. You phoned . . ."

"Oh . . . oh, yes. I must apologize. My hours are most irregular. I'm turning into something of a night owl. Forgive me."

"Of course. I just didn't want you to think I'd ignored your call. I knocked on your door several times, and when I got no answer, I decided the call might be a mistake."

"So sorry. I was wondering if you'd made your decision."

"I have. I'd like very much to handle the work you outlined."

"Good. And I'm sure you'll do a fine job. Are you free at the moment?"

"Quite free."

"Then I suggest you drop up here. We can arrange the final details."

The final details. They surprised me. Jasper King paced the floor while he briefed me. He revealed what was close to anger—certainly frustration. But nothing abnormal; nothing more exceptional than the reactions of an executive whose affairs had been going badly.

"Miss Spain, it must be understood that you are in complete charge. Your job is to inspect, appraise, and rearrange as you see fit. You are not to be impeded in any way."

Striving to get his exact meaning, I said, "I've noticed much of great value in the castle. Not paintings, necessarily . . ."

87

"That's exactly what I mean."

"As an example, there is an exquisite French writing desk in my room that is being used as a serving table."

"And you'll find more of that. Much more. I want it stopped. I'm to blame, of course. When I left my place on Long Island . . ."

He stopped suddenly, just as I expected further information on his tragedy, on the understandable disruption springing from the loss of his wife at a time when business reverses were bludgeoning him from all sides.

This was forthcoming only to a limited extent—this when he pierced me with what was almost a glare. Then his expression softened into what I could only define as a *lost* look.

"You're a great deal like her—your hair, your appearance."

I did not know what to say. He obviously assumed that I was aware of his personal tragedy. But then again, perhaps not. He could have been speaking for himself, *within* himself, seeing me as an objective reflection rather than a person. At any rate, I found that I did not want his confidence. A vague, instinctive warning told me to be careful. So I settled for a "thank you," and waited.

"She is very beautiful, you know."

"I'm sure."

Fortunately, the interlude was over. He reverted to the crisp executive, saying, "I want the abuse of my valuable pieces stopped. You must see to it."

"I'll certainly do my best."

All in all, I came away from the interview with mixed thoughts and new questions. His anger at the misuse of his treasures should have reflected against the thoughtless guests who were misusing them. Still, none of them were being asked to leave or even being reprimanded directly. Did this prove the sense of responsibility for their welfare to which Jeff Stone had alluded? It seemed to.

I found personal disappointment in the fact that the objects of my true interest—Jasper King's collection of more priceless treasures, his master oils—had not been stressed. Did this mean that they had already been put out of harm's way? I had not been told specifically that they were not under my jurisdiction, so I assumed I'd been left to find them if I could. A kind of hide-and-seek game I did not necessarily wish to play.

But to compensate for all else, there was the confidence Jasper King had placed in me. I'd come to Caliban's Castle with little chance of even being admitted. Now, here I was with an exciting assignment and authority that put me above all others except perhaps Callie White. Callie had been cordial and helpful, and I expected no trouble from her, but even she, I felt, would be required to bow to my wishes if it came to a conflict of interests.

However, a certain wariness arose from this thought. What if Callie turned out to be more devious than she seemed? Could she possibly have been the recipient of Jasper King's impassioned verses there in the tower? From what I'd seen of her, I could not believe it. But I was fast learning to take nothing for granted in Caliban's Castle. It seemed to be a place where one incongruity was piled on another, until the overlapping of fact and fantasy left all decisions subject to change at a moment's notice.

A fine example of this occurred immediately after I went downstairs from my interview with Jasper King, when I walked out into the square and found Jeff Stone examining an ancient crossbow. He was booted and jacketed for the outdoors and had a container of arrows over his shoulder.

He greeted me with a quizzical expression. "Any idea how this thing works, precious?"

"None whatever. What do you propose to do with it?"

"Hunt."

"Hunt what—rabbits?"

"Bear."

"Jeff. Don't tell me! Is this another of those silly dares?"

"As I said, a person can become bored. . . ."

"Then why don't you leave? Go back to the city, where you can find any number of things to interest you."

He blinked at my sudden flare of anger. In fact, I was surprised myself.

"Easy, pet," Jeff said. "This isn't like walking the parapet. I've got a pretty lethal toy here. It goes like this."

With that, he fitted an arrow into the clumsy contraption and pointed it at the heavy wooden upright of the entrance gate. By sheer chance he aimed true, and the short-shafted arrow buried itself several inches into the wood.

"How's that? You can call me Robin Hood, pet. And I'm loaded for bear."

"You're actually going to hunt the beast? A bear is dangerous! It could tear you to pieces."

He was in a gay mood, forced perhaps. " 'Not I,' said the sparrow. 'Not with my trusty bow and arrow.' " And with that he trooped off across the drawbridge, leaving me more frustrated than I had any right to be.

So I prayerfully consigned Jeff to the protection of the patron saint of fools, but that was not the end of it. The incident put me in a mood that stayed with me for the whole afternoon.

In search of Callie White, I went down into the kitchen for the first time, following the route along which I'd seen the waitresses on the staff bring food up to the dining hall. It was a low-ceilinged, spacious place with barred windows high in the wall above the level of the moat. It looked to have been constructed originally as the liege lord's prison. There were marks indicating that extensive remodeling had been done, where walls of individual cells had been torn out to create one large room, which had been converted in turn into a kitchen with modern appliances rather than the primitive ovens and open fires of medieval times. A logical concession to modern comfort.

There were four of the kitchen staff in sight, two men—one in a tall cook's cap—and two girls, but they were busy at the far end of the room, and I found Callie's small office just at the foot of the stairway.

She sat at a desk and looked up from what she was doing. "Karen! So you're up and about? Some lunch?"

"I think I'll wait for dinner. In the meantime, I'm going to have a look around."

"A little exploring?"

"You might call it that. I've accepted Mr. King's proposition and want to get right at it. Tell me, where are the guest rooms located?"

"They are all on the second level. Most of them on your side."

91

"Another thing. Was there any furniture in the castle before Jasper King moved up here?"

"Yes. A lot of it not fit to use. It's on the side opposite you—most of it."

"Why was it removed from the rooms and so many of Mr. King's fine pieces put into use?"

Callie shrugged. "Things were pretty casual when that gang arrived. To some extent, they furnished their own quarters. The only people Jasper brought with him are over there. Real professionals."

She waved in the direction of the kitchen staff, hard at their jobs of giving the best possible culinary service.

"Callie," I said, "let me be frank. Do you feel that the job Mr. King has given me overlaps what you've been assigned to do?"

"Not at all," she replied cordially. "I'm here to try to integrate the castle. I think he wants to get it running smoothly for the future. I'm sure there will be other guests." She paused to grimace in distaste. "Less irresponsible ones. I suppose I should have paid more attention to the furniture. But I'm glad to have you take the chore off my hands."

That did not exactly answer my question as to the allocation of authority. Did she still see herself as in complete charge, with me as an assistant?

I decided not to press the matter, thus leaving the situation to be resolved in action rather than agreement.

I said, "You promised me a helper or two. . . ."

"Of course. I have a crew of gardeners working in the park. Local people. I'll have a couple of them meet you by the fountain. I assume you plan to get right to it?"

"I'd like to begin as soon as possible."

We went upstairs together, and a few minutes later

Callie returned from the outside with two men. One was middle-aged, grizzled, his gnarled hands indicating years of manual labor. He was introduced merely as Tom. The other, Lee, was younger and looked of the same type though less scarred. They had one thing in common—the tight-lipped taciturnity attributed to the native New Englander, a cast into which Callie White herself did not fit. They were the type I felt a true English overlord would have referred to as "good dogs," faithful, uncomplaining, unquestioning.

"First," I told them, "we'll check the old furniture and then make a few changes."

Thus began what turned out to be a most interesting afternoon.

13

There was a wealth of run-of-the-mill furniture piled in two of the suites across the square from the tenanted side of the castle on the second level, and in the beginning I had no difficulty, because I refurnished my own rooms, replacing the French writing desk with a serviceable table, and two Chippendale lyre-backed chairs with a battered pair of maple straight-backs.

The bed was a problem. I finally decided to leave it, as it would be less abused in my room than in storage, and its size was formidable.

The John Pimm highboy went next, no great loss to me, because the gaudy panels grated on my sensibilities anyhow. I left the lovely girandole clock as a touch of luxury in what would be a shabbily furnished room. The Egyptian chairs went also, replaced by a battered overstuffed lounge that had seen better days.

We were so busy that I scarcely had time to realize how much I was enjoying the work, the association with the lovely pieces the like of which I had seen only in museums. Also, there was the satisfaction of saving them from ruin.

Either through Callie White's good offices or the thoughtfulness of the culinary staff, a maid arrived with a tray just as we finished with my quarters—a pitcher of iced lemonade and a glass filled with a colorless liquid that I took to be water.

I was wrong. The older of my two helpers, Tom, picked up the glass with obvious relish and downed the contents. He smacked his lips afterward and broke his stoic silence. "Tennessee moonshine, miss. One-twenty proof. Our afternoon break."

I covered my gasp with a sip of lemonade. That meant the stuff was practically straight alcohol, and he'd downed it without a quiver. This proved two things to me: that the Volstead Act did not interfere with the drinking habits of some of these people, and that they did not pamper themselves. They drank like he-men. I wondered nervously if I would now have an inebriated assistant on my hands, but the worry was unfounded in fact. The generous beaker of liquid dynamite had no effect upon Tom whatever.

With my quarters done over, I continued with my mandate, knocking on the first door I came to in the resident wing. It was open, and I was greeted by a scowl on an otherwise pretty face.

"What do *you* want?"

We had met before. Ginger Wade, the girl who had seen me as trying to take Rory Talbott away from her during the armor-removing episode.

"I've come to change the furnishings," I said.

That deepened the scowl. "What are you talking about?"

"Some of Mr. King's finer pieces are being abused. We're making some changes."

"Well, of all the pious, long-nosed busybodies . . ."

We might have had a further argument there at the door if something inside hadn't caught my attention. Smoke curling lazily upward.

More sharply angered myself now, I pushed past her and rushed to where a cigarette, placed on the edge of a lovely Pembroke rosewood table, was about to inflict a wound. Marring that gleaming surface would have been sacrilege.

I snatched up the cigarette. "Is this yours?"

"Yes, it's mine. Are we supposed to stop smoking, on top of everything else?"

"You're supposed to be civilized!" I looked about. "You don't even have an ashtray. Is this the way you treat your things at home?"

I noted only in passing that she was not alone. Rory Talbott was sprawling lazily on a Sheraton sofa that belonged in a roped-off section of some museum. He was watching the encounter with interest but hadn't moved.

Ginger Wade stood poised like a small tigress ready to spring, and perhaps I would have been physically attacked if I hadn't remained on the offensive. I motioned to my two helpers, who were standing in the doorway.

"Take that table first. Then come back for the sofa."

They moved in, bulking up my presence in the room, so to speak, and Ginger hesitated. As they picked up the table, I went to where Rory was sitting.

"Have you been putting your feet on that nee-dlepoint?" I demanded.

He slid guiltily off the sofa and backed away. "Me? No. I've just been sitting here."

It flashed into my mind that the two of them were probably living together in that suite, but I could not have cared less. "Even sitting on it is out of bounds," I told him.

Ginger was thrown off-balance by the entrance of my aides, and reacted by doing the womanly thing. She burst into tears.

"Rory! Don't just stand there! Throw these people out! They can't just walk in here and take our furniture!"

"They seem to be doing it," he murmured uncertainly.

I said, "You won't be left sitting on the floor. You'll find plenty of less valuable pieces in the rooms across the square."

It had been my plan to remove and replace, but in this case I changed my mind. These two indolents could get their own. That might keep them too busy to do mad things such as challenging Jeff Stone to risk his life on balustrades and bear hunts.

Completely frustrated now, Ginger threw herself on another sofa and continued to bawl. I left her to her sorrow, because that particular piece was quite shabby and of no great value.

"I guess that does it," I said after my movers had made three trips. "As I said, you will find . . ."

Ginger raised her head and tried to kill me with a look. She said, "You wait! Just wait till I tell Jasper what you did! You'll go out of here so fast your head'll spin!"

I had a disquieting thought. What if Ginger was the one, the girl who had been listening to Jasper King's love verses there in the tower? Grotesque, but not impossible. She seemed very sure of her power, and she had the youth, the verve, the beauty, that men seeking lost youth are likely to yearn for.

If true, did Jasper King know he was sharing her with Rory Talbott?

"I'm making these changes on Mr. King's direct orders," I assured her, and went on to the next suite.

The rest of the afternoon was disappointing so far as retrieving abused furniture was concerned. I was vague about the number of younger guests in the castle, having met none of them, but I found that they occupied four suites in all. I found a valuable chair on my next visit, and took a Sir William Beechey oil painting off another wall, but only for the reason that the sun hit it each afternoon, and it would eventually be bleached.

One thing disappointed me. I had hoped to find some of Jasper King's truly priceless oils hanging about in the guest rooms. There were none. Only a few cheap prints and the Chinese silk screen of Fujiyama that had once been beautiful but was now so badly worn as to be without value.

So I finished the chore by sending Lee to search out Callie White. He returned with my order—an armful of sheets we used to cover the pieces. Then we called it a day.

It was still quite early, and I wandered toward the open square, thinking to cross the drawbridge into the outer gardens for a breath of cooler air.

I was intercepted by Jeff Stone at the foot of the stairway on the first level and boorishly took out the last of my day's anger upon him.

He smiled cheerfully as he approached. "Not a hair of the bear," he announced. "The brute must have heard I was coming and headed for the mountains."

I eyed him coldly. "I wonder if you realize how idiotically childish you look carrying that silly crossbow?"

With that I turned and retraced my way upward for no reason other than a haughty retreat. He did not follow me. When I reached the second level, I looked back and was somewhat ashamed of myself. He looked like a forlorn little boy who had been scolded by an adult, with no idea of what he'd done wrong. I almost surrendered to the tender feeling that swept me, then steeled myself and walked on, angered anew by the effect he had on me. I flatly refused to fall in love with an immature wastrel with no idea of where he was going in life.

As a buffer, I deliberately dragged Max Bowman into my mind and began extolling his virtues. Stable, even-tempered, kind and considerate, ambitious and industrious.

Until I was forced to acknowledge my own childishness, and ended the mental soliloquy by demanding to know why love and common sense invariably remained strangers to each other.

Of course, there was no answer.

And it was at that moment that the most interesting adventure of my busy day began. I found myself on the upper level of the castle, where I'd previously visited with Callie White as a guide—a cool and breezy place to calm my spirits. Then I looked out across the moor and again saw that distant kneeling figure at the graveside of Caliban Leach and his Agala.

My reaction was quick and totally impulsive. I hurried down the stairs, into the outer gardens, and off across the moor with a single hope in mind—that I could reach the bluffs in time.

I succeeded. The figure remained kneeling as I approached, intent upon the work at hand, not seeing me. I was within a hundred yards of the graves when the mysterious person—a young man—came to his feet, saw me, and took several quick retreating steps toward the bluff.

I raised my hand in what I hoped was a friendly gesture and slowed my pace. He hesitated, then decided to wait and face me.

My first impression, striking or not, was of a Botticelli cherub grown to young manhood. Perhaps my day's battles had made me oversensitive, but what I saw was an inner beauty that transcended the masculine, a perfection that appeared to radiate from within. The physical perfection was there: a slim body; dark, windblown hair; creamily tan, flawless skin; and two dark eyes as deep as bottomless wells.

Now that I'd arrived, I could think of nothing to say. "Hello. I saw you before, and came over, but you were gone." I finally managed that, and tried to look totally casual.

"I'm not doing any harm."

"Of course not. I'm Karen Spain. I just wanted to meet the person tending these graves. It's such a thoughtful thing to do."

"We do it every year."

"I'm sure Mr. King would be happy to know that."

"Mr. King?"

"He's the man living in the castle."

"We never go there. We just come here to see to the graves."

"You haven't told me your name."

"Paul Davernne."

I insisted on shaking hands. He complied timidly. His first fears—because of trespassing, I supposed— were now less apparent.

"When I came before, I wondered where you'd vanished to. I looked down onto the beach, but you weren't there."

"I was in the cave."

"Oh? I didn't know there was a cave down there."

"It leads to the castle."

"How interesting. Would you like to show me?"

He was uncertain about that. "The path is kind of dangerous."

"I'm sure I can manage it with you to help me."

"All right. If you want to."

I'd been overly effusive, an attitude that did not become me, but I hadn't wanted to frighten him away as before. We reached the foot of the bluff without mishap, and I tried to correct my image by being more myself.

I said, "Paul, you still haven't told me who you are and why you come here. I *would* like to know." With that I moved toward one of the larger boulders and sat down. He followed and sat down in the sand in front of me, apparently willing, though still reluctant, to be questioned.

"We don't hurt anyone," he repeated. "All we do is fix the graves."

"You say *we*. Is someone with you?"

"Not this time. My sister came last year and the year before. But she got married, and now I come alone."

It took some time to get his story. It came out in monosyllabic replies to my questions, during which time I discovered that if you wanted to know about Paul Davernne you had to ask. He volunteered nothing, yet answered me openly and honestly. And I gained a smug satisfaction in learning things that Callie White, the local historian, did not know. One thing she'd told me was verified—that the American courts, at the behest of Neville Leach, had treated the children of Caliban and Agala badly. The court had found for the English relatives in every detail, leaving the blood daughter, Madelaine, completely out, because no record of marriage was ever found to prove that Madelaine, the mother of Paul and his sister, was not born out of wedlock. The verdict, from what I could learn, was accepted with a surprising lack of bitterness. Madelaine married Angel Davernne, and tending the graves at the castle became a duty of Paul and his sister, Inez, as a result of a deathbed vow to their mother some ten years previously. Evidently the neglect had weighed on her conscience. The surprising thing to me was the fact that the grave-tending went unnoticed for so long. It spoke of the castle tenants' lack of interest in the outer reaches of the estate, with Callie White herself included. That in turn strengthened another idea that had been shaping in my mind—that those who came to live in Caliban's Castle never stayed very long, never long enough to become familiar with the entire establishment.

As the sun lowered, I continued to delve into Paul Davernne's affairs. "What do you and your sister do, Paul? How do you make your living?"

"Inez is a nurse. She works in a New York hospital. I tend bar in a Manhattan speakeasy."

That last shocked me. Even though we were close to the same age, Paul had aroused my maternal instincts, and I saw his occupation much as a mother might view her son entering a life of crime.

He went on. "It looks like Prohibition will be repealed if Roosevelt gets in, and I think he will. Then I'll have to find something else to do."

"Do you think people will stop drinking if it becomes legal?"

"No. I guess they'll keep right on."

Not wishing to get into a political discussion, I said, "You mentioned hiding in the caves."

"Yes."

"Would you like to show me?"

He brightened, and I congratulated myself on breaking through to him. Most of his reluctance had vanished—to the point where he seemed ready to communicate without being cross-examined.

"I've got a little warm place in there where I stay, but all the caves and tunnels are warm except one. I can show you."

"I'd like that."

Paul produced two flashlights just inside the tunnel entrance into which he'd disappeared that time of my first visit. This was my first experience with a cave, and this one was awesome—blackness so thick that the flash beams had little effect. They merely bored feeble channels through the ebony wall to assure us there was no obstacle immediately ahead.

Paul turned his beam to the left a little way in. "That's where I live when I'm up here."

I saw a cozy little nook with a rock shelf where he could put his sleeping bag, which he used as a mattress. The thermal warmth made bedding unnecessary. An orange crate was his table, and he'd fastened a small crucifix to the wall.

"My country place." He grinned.

We moved on through the twisting, meandering passageways. I said, "Paul, we won't get lost, will we?"

His laugh was comforting as he replied, "Not a chance. I explore to pass the time, and I know practically all of the caves. I told you I never go to the castle, but that wasn't true. I meant I don't go there when someone's using it. The place was empty for a while. Even then, I almost got caught."

"By a ghost?"

"No. A woman. She was dressed like a man, but she was pretty. She was in the big open square writing in a book. I stumbled on the stairs, and she looked up, but she didn't see me."

Callie White, no doubt, during one of her investigations at the castle.

Paul's tones turned more solemn now. "Maybe you didn't know, but my grandmother came here to hide before the Civil War, or about that time. The castle was only partly built then, and they hid runaway slaves on their way to Canada in the caves."

"But your grandmother stayed and married Caliban Leach."

"She didn't marry him."

"No, but I'm sure they considered themselves married. What do you know about your grandfather?"

"He suffered a lot. All his life. He was a cripple, you see, and he was in pain most of the time. The only relief he got was from what Grandmother Agala did. She knew *arrêt* and *traitement*, and she could help him."

"In what way?"

Arrêt is Haitian magic—spells against the evil spirits in my grandfather's body that twisted him up in the first place. *Traitement* is using herbs and different magic charms. She sent to Haiti and got the plants she needed and put them in the garden in the square."

"She must have loved him a great deal."

"She couldn't help it," Paul said simply. "He saved her life and gave her something to live for." To him, that was the complete answer.

Remembering the crucifix on the alcove wall, I said, "Are you Catholic, Paul?"

"Yes."

Again the simplicity, the honesty—while I wondered how Haitian voodoo could be satisfactorily merged with the tenets of the Roman Catholic faith. Evidently it had been done.

As we continued to push through the winding labyrinth, I was not diverted, because there was nothing to see—only the tunnel, with occasional intersections, where Paul was never in doubt as to our route.

I said, "Paul, did you ever hear of an Englishman named Neville Leach?"

"Sure. He came over here after Grandfather died and took his money back to England—or at least a lot of it—plus what he got from selling the castle."

"He didn't take all the money?"

"No. Just what Grandfather thought they ought to have over there. He planned everything, and there was enough to take care of my grandmother and my mother. When Grandmother Agala died, there was still enough to set my father up in business."

"Then you weren't left penniless."

"Oh, no. Grandfather Leach put our money where nobody but my grandmother could find it."

"Then you and your sister are fairly well off?"

Paul laughed as though recalling a joke. "No. My father wasn't a very good businessman. He went bankrupt."

I didn't pry any further. Another thought had struck me. I said, "You told me all the caves and tunnels were warm except one. Why is that?"

"The ice."

"The ice?"

"We're almost there. I'll show you."

We traveled another two or three hundred yards, and I experienced the physical effect of what appeared to be a phenomenon—a cave where the thermal heat did not penetrate. The cave was large, high-ceilinged, and my first look into it left me confused. It appeared to be filled with glittering stars, tiny pinpoints of beautiful varicolored lights thrown back at our flashlight beams.

"What on earth is it?" I gasped.

"Ice. Can't you see it? The whole cave is filled with ice blocks mostly covered with sawdust to keep them from melting too fast."

"But where did it come from?"

"The ponds on the land around the castle. They cut the ice into blocks in the winter and brought it in here."

My guess concerning Jasper King's cool tower had been wrong. Back in New York City there had been talk about a new industry—air-conditioning. Some people thought it might well pull the nation out of the depression. Using the same principles by which refrigerators were built, it was said that whole rooms could be cooled, entire apartments, even buildings. Much of that was still in the future, but it had occurred to me that with wealthy people always able to fill their needs, Jasper King had installed one of the units.

As it was now proved, he relied on nature for his comfort against the heat of the thermal fault. Blocks of ice.

"But how do they get it up into the castle?" I asked.

Paul moved his flash beam. "That tunnel rises more than the others. It leads to a stairway up into the northeast corner of the castle. I guess they just carry the blocks up."

One thing was evident. Jasper King shared his comfort with no one but the mysterious ladylove to whom he recited romantic verses.

Paul said, "We're right under the castle now. Here, I'll show you."

He led me along another tunnel, and we came shortly into an even larger cave. I tried to carve its dimensions out of the darkness with my flash beam, while Paul used his on a tour-guide basis.

"That long block there. They did ceremonies on it."

"The red stains look like old blood."

"I guess maybe they killed animals," he admitted with reluctance.

Only animals, I hoped.

His beam traced a floor pattern near the opposite wall. "That's a map of the planets."

"An astrological star. Those marks indicate the houses. Was your grandmother an astrologer?"

"I guess so."

I got the impression that he did not care to talk about that aspect of Agala's life. "How did they light this cave for their ceremonies?"

"With pitch torches. There's a box of them over there. We can light one if you want to."

"Let's not. It's like a Turkish bath down here. I'd rather find a cooler place."

"That's because the heat rises out of the earth right behind the altar. I'll show you."

He led me behind the rectangular stone block, and I saw the irregular fissure in the wall.

"It's an open shaft that goes down and down. I guess . . . maybe into an old volcano."

That was hardly a comforting thought! Even more frightening because of the sounds from below. There, at the very mouth of the shaft, the hissing as from serpents heard in the courtyard above deepened into more powerful threats, a rhythmic surge of sound, as though the invisible shaft were the throat of a monster gasping for air to fill mammoth lungs, blasting out hot breath to sear the timid and warn even the bravest that the beast below was merely biding its time.

I was far from being the bravest. "I've had all of this I can take, Paul. Let's go back."

"You won't have to," he replied. "There's a stairway just inside that tunnel mouth there. It leads up into the big dining room with the fireplace."

"Come with me. I'm sure Callie White would like to meet you—even Mr. King himself."

The shake of his head was a positive refusal. "I'll go back. I'm leaving tomorrow morning after I water the plants. I've been away from my job too long."

"Paul . . . I want to see you again. I want to meet your sister. I live in New York. . . ."

"My sister works at the Melrose Hospital."

"I'll remember."

In sudden warmth, I kissed Paul on the cheek, our short acquaintance notwithstanding. He was like a breath of fresh air in comparison to the spoiled, confused coterie I'd found in Caliban's Castle.

I went up the stairway he'd indicated and found a narrow door at the top. I opened it slowly and found myself in the great hall near the fireplace. One of the maids was present, no one else, and she was on the way to the kitchen stairs with her back to me. I didn't know quite why I acted so furtively, but furtiveness seemed to blend with the dour castle, to be a part of its silent, menacing mood.

I crossed into the square and up the stairs toward my quarters. All I wanted from life at the moment was a cool shower and an hour's rest.

There was a note on the table I'd substituted for the

French writing desk: "Dinner at ten in my rooms? Jasper King."

In my present physical and mental state, I was somewhat less than thrilled.

I did wonder if it was an invitation or a tactfully worded command.

14

Upon awakening quite refreshed, my first thought was of an apology, one I owed to Jeff Stone. I'd treated him shabbily. So after slipping into a light summer print and seeing to my makeup, I knocked on the door of his bedroom off the common room.

His "Come in" was grumpy, and there was a pout on his handsome face when I confronted him. "Something I can do for you?" he asked as he went on with what he was doing—fussing with that stupid crossbow.

I resolved not to let it bother me. "Jeff, I'm sorry for the way I acted. I had no right to carp at you."

He shrugged. "It's okay. Would you like a drink?"

"Nothing hard. I could do with a glass of cold lemonade."

"Then let's go down and order it."

"Do you think we'll be safe if we go unarmed?"

After a quick frown, he accepted that as a joke. "You never can tell. That blasted bear may have come in for an early dinner."

"That's all right. If we find him at one of the tables, we'll sit with him and make friends. Did you find any tracks when you were out hunting?"

"I went to where he attacked one of the local people. The bushes were all smashed. You could see where he'd dragged the man he killed."

I shuddered. "Jeff, if you must go after the animal, please take a gun. Take the sort of high-powered rifle hunters use on such animals."

"That wouldn't be fair."

"Fair to whom—the idiots who challenged you, the bear, or to me?"

"Why should you care?"

"Will you stop repeating that question? I do care."

Before he could reply, we entered the dining hall. Ginger Wade was seated at one of the tables with two of the other girls. They were drinking from tall, frosty-looking glasses.

Jeff turned in that direction, and I followed him, whereupon the group, after a whispered word from Ginger, got up and moved to the opposite side of the room.

We selected a table and sat down. Jeff stared after them, mystified. "What did I do *now*?"

"It isn't you. Ginger would like to have *my* scalp. I took the furniture out of her room. She's mad."

He turned his stare on me. "You . . . what?"

"I guess you haven't heard. Jasper King gave me the job of salvaging his valuable pieces. They were spread around in the guest rooms, and I gathered them up. Ginger was hit hardest."

"You've seen Jasper?"

"Yes. We're getting on quite well together."

Through whatever mysterious process they'd devised, a waitress appeared from the basement and came to our table. Through habit more than anything else, I ordered lemonade. Jeff ordered Scotch and water. The waitress left. Jeff reached out and took my hand. He said, "Precious, there's a table out there in the garden. The atmosphere is better out there."

I had no objection, so when the drinks were delivered, we left the great hall and Jeff led me into the jungle in the open square. I hadn't really explored it, and I was pleasantly surprised at what I now found.

An idyllic spot sheltered on all sides by jungle growth. By chance, there was a moon overhead—by chance, but an urge for the romantic suggested to me that it had been foreordained. The yellow rays beamed down on a plot of soft grass, a small table, two chairs, and a chaise longue. The heady perfume could have been too much in the light of day, but now it seemed appropriate.

Jeff set down his glass. He put mine beside it, then took my hands in his. "Karen," he whispered, "I love you."

It would have been so easy to reply in kind, and I tried to. I realized that I'd been waiting for him to say that from the very beginning. But the blocks remained; the need to qualify and weigh and measure.

As he drew me into his arms and kissed me, I did not resist. He drew back and looked into my eyes. "I'd hoped you could say the same," he whispered.

Oh, yes . . . yes . . . I can, darling! I do love you. You opened up a new world for me. Don't go away. Don't ever go away. . . .

It was my heart talking, not my lips. My heart trying to break through the barrier around it and come free.

Again I was in Jeff's arms, wanting to stay there forever, eager for the rising passion of his kiss, wanting to respond.

Not able.

The barrier weakened and trembled. But stayed.

His withdrawal was simultaneous with the darkening of a cloud passing over the moon. Darkness. Then, when the yellow rays came on again, he'd picked up his glass and was handing me mine.

"Maybe if it was a little stronger than lemonade. . . ?"

"Jeff, please . . . I do care . . ."

His manner changed to the more serious as he drew me down on the chaise longue. "Karen, darling . . . you'll do something for me?"

"Of course. Anything I can."

"You're in very strong with Jasper King."

"I wouldn't say that."

"But you can see him anytime you want to."

"I suppose so. Anyone can. He's on the intercom . . ."

"Oh, no, anyone can't. He sees no one but those he favors. You . . . Callie White."

"But he liked you. He gave you an airplane."

"On the spur of the moment. As a matter of fact, precious, I think Jasper's going off his rocker. I think his tremendous losses have affected his mind."

"That's a terrible thing to say. A man of his stature . . ."

"That's the point. His stature. Look at it this way. Suppose you were so wealthy that priceless oil paintings and the other valuable artifacts around here—rare furniture and such—were secondary items in your itinerary."

"They *aren't* secondary!"

"All right. Then why does he have to have an inventory? Because he paid so little attention to them. Is that the way you treat things that are important to you?"

"But he's been so busy. He lost his wife . . ."

"And the bulk of his fortune all at one time. The point is . . ."

"Just what is the point, Jeff?"

"That I'm stone broke, precious. And I owe money to some very stuffy people."

"How much money?"

114

"So much that if I'd sold the Snipe, which I intended to do, it would only have staved them off for a while. Now I haven't even got the Snipe."

"I'm sure they would understand and give you more time."

"They're not understanding chaps. They collect their debts with clubs. A broken arm is only warning that they might get really violent."

"I have a little money saved, darling."

"You've got more than that. You have the means of saving my life."

"You know I'll do anything I can . . ."

"Jasper's paintings."

"Oh, Jeff! No! Without the money, they'll give you time."

He plunged on desperately. "They won't, Karen. But even if they did, it wouldn't help. There's no place on earth I can get the money."

"You're asking me to *steal* Jasper King's property!"

"No! I'm not. I'm only asking you to tell me where the paintings are. No one seems to know. They're hidden somewhere in the castle. Just tell me where."

"And then close my eyes."

"Sweetheart! He doesn't even know how many he's got! Would one grubby little masterpiece mean anything to him? Something he didn't even know he owned?"

"Jeff, you say he won't talk to you. I think I can help there. I'm dining with him tonight. I'll ask him to see you, and when you tell him the truth I'm sure he'll be generous."

"In other words, you're telling me to go to the devil."

"Jeff, I'm not!"

"Never mind! Forget it. Forget the whole thing!"

With that, he threw his glass into the jungle and rushed off.

I remained where I was, my heart crying within me. His kiss, his arms about me—all of it had meant nothing, only a part of his act, a device to gain my help in robbing Jasper King.

Never in my life had I been more miserable, more depressed. I was certainly in fine shape to meet Jasper King!

After indulging in the self-pity of a few tears, I dried my eyes and grimly told myself that I'd really lost nothing. In fact, I'd gained something—the proof that my wariness in not surrendering to my emotions was wise.

But emotions can be stubborn, and as I went back to my quarters to repair my makeup before seeing Jasper King, I had visions of Jeff's tragic face before he'd rushed off. If his love for me had been false, his fear of creditors had not. And in love, did not one accept another for better or for worse?

I sternly rejected that line of weakness and hurried to Jasper King's mysterious northeast tower. . . .

15

"Kathleen Mavourneen, the gray dawn is break-ing . . ."

The soft, sweet voice was coming down from the tower as I timidly entered Jasper King's quarters after knocking twice. It was as it had been before—the tower door ajar, Jasper King not in sight.

There was one change. He had not forgotten his dinner invitation. A table was set for two, luxuriously appointed, with a long-stemmed rose set in the center between two tall, slim tapers.

The opposite door, the one into the anteroom under the tower, was open also, and the singing was coming down from above.

Halfway through the pause, and in a speaking voice evidently that of the singer, "Wouldn't you like something more cheerful, darling?"

Jasper King replied, "If you say so, darling."

"I'm sorry. I know it's your favorite."

And the song went on. She had a beautiful voice, whoever she was. I tried to identify her as Ginger Wade, recalling that one's threat. It could have been the girl, but the acoustics were such that I could not be sure one way or the other. The tower formation and my comparatively remote listening post gave a slightly tinny effect.

Still, the voice was appealing, and all in all I found myself enjoying it—not only the song, but the cooling effect of what I now knew were the ice blocks Jasper King used to temper the thermal heat from below.

The singing stopped now, and I heard footsteps at the top of the steel ladder. My retreat was headlong and undignified, but it took me out into the corridor, where I waited a reasonable time and then knocked.

Jasper King came to admit me. The singing had stopped, and in a sense I was seeing a different man than I had met previously. He was pleasant, brisk, and more sharply businesslike.

"Miss Spain! How good of you to come. I hope you have a good appetite. I've ordered a special dinner."

He gave an order over the house phone and then pressed a drink upon me—a fine vintage wine, so he said, although I had no way of knowing. However, the bottle certainly looked authentic with its French label and dusty appearance.

Two from the domestic staff served the dinner, so rigidly proper that we could have been in one of the finest restaurants in Manhattan; an amazing display of gourmet food. Green turtle soup, something I had tasted but once before in my life; pheasant under glass, entirely new to my middle-class existence; an avocado salad; and fresh strawberries in rich cream.

I would have been less astounded had I not known of his ice supply. And there was probably a refrigerator of the latest design somewhere in the kitchen.

During the meal I was tempted to ask a reckless question: The lady in the tower—why did she not join us? I resisted, though, and continued to wonder about her.

"I understand you have been doing a fine job in straightening out the place," he said.

Presuming that Callie White had reported to him, I replied, "I've moved the valuable furniture out of the rooms where it was being used and had the pieces covered. There is more that should be done, though. The heat. The humidity in the castle will eventually do damage."

"Don't distress yourself. I have been making some plans."

"I'm glad. That condition applies even more so to any valuable art you have. So far, I've found none. Are your paintings here in the castle?"

"The paintings? Oh, yes. They are here in the third level. I'll give you the key. My more valuable works are still in the packing cases. I'd like you to check them and give me an inventory. Then return them to the cases. I'll be leaving the castle shortly."

He had a brightness of eye, an almost feverish glow in manner and appearance that made me uneasy. "Will you be returning to the city?"

His expression turned grim. "Much to their distress. They tried to ruin me. That was their mistake. Now they'll have to pay."

I assumed *they* were his business enemies. "Do you think the depression is about over?"

"Perhaps, but that makes little difference. Breaking markets create millionaires as well as rising markets. I've been planning, getting ready. Now I am about to move."

"Then I'd better get your artworks ready. Will you want the furniture packed?"

"No need for you to bother about that. We'll call a moving company when the time comes, and they'll take care of everything. There's something else I want you to do."

His eyes were even brighter now. Without moving perceptibly, he looked to be ready to pounce, and I found myself measuring the distance to the door.

"I want you to be my eyes and my ears."

"I don't understand. I . . ."

"There are enemies all around."

"Do you mean here in the castle?"

"No one is as they appear. Enemies assume many disguises."

For a few moments I thought he was referring to me—trying to pierce *my* disguise. But then he smiled and softened.

"I don't wish to frighten you. You are in no danger. I merely want you to watch everyone in the castle and report to me regularly."

"If you feel that way, there must be certain people whom you suspect."

"Yes, but they're clever."

"You certainly don't suspect Miss White."

"No, but watch her. Watch her carefully."

"That group of young people? They hardly appear sinister."

"Some of them feel they have reason, I'm sure. But this castle is huge. Others could be lurking about. People we never see."

The fever in him was becoming more tangible. I searched desperately for an excuse to get away.

"I'll do what I can. But in the meantime, there is my other job—getting things ready . . ."

"Of course, of course. The paintings. I want an inventory and an estimate of their value. Here is the key to the storeroom."

"I'll get to it immediately," I said as he took a key off his ring and handed it to me.

"It's the third door down the corridor to your right as you go out. And now, for our nightcap. A little brandy?"

I wanted to refuse, but when he called it a nightcap, it implied a finish to our evening. It *was* finished—and quicker than I expected—when Jasper King set down the bottle without pouring, looked toward the tower door, and assumed a listening pose.

His whole attention went in that direction, to the extent that he forgot my presence. He hurried across the room and left me standing there.

This time, he closed the tower door behind him. I crossed over and strained my ear against the panel, and in a few moments I heard what possibly had come to his sharper ears earlier. Soft feminine laughter.

I waited, not knowing what to do. Should I remain in the room until he returned? I had never before experienced such erratic behavior, which added to my confusion.

Then the decision was taken from me. A high cry of anguish came down from the tower. I stood there, frozen, as it was repeated. Muted by the closed door, it sounded more male than female.

I fled from the room. . . .

16

A confidant.

Someone to talk to. Someone to advise me. This was imperative. Either that or pack my bag and run from the castle as precipitously as I had fled Jasper King's rooms.

I reached my own quarters and sought to quiet my abused nerves before making any decision one way or another. A little quiet reasoning, I told myself, would certainly help the situation. I realized that I would be biased in my attitude toward Jasper King, because he was my benefactor. Therefore I was inclined to excuse a great deal—to call his actions eccentric in order to combat the vague feeling that he was mad as a hatter.

And possibly worse? Was he keeping a girl prisoner in that tower? What sort of abuse did those screams indicate? All of which roiled through my mind.

Suddenly I wanted very much to be near Jeff Stone—but to feel his arms around me more so than to ask his advice and abide by his judgments. At this point I forcefully realized the poverty of being in love with an unstable man. If only I could have put Max Bowman's level head on Jeff's handsome shoulder and had the best of both.

I wanted very much now to put the whole matter aside for later consideration. With only the singing and the laughter, I had been able to do that. But those cries of pain put upon me an obligation to investigate, or to at least consult with someone whose advice might help me. I thought of calling Max. No good. The intercom in my room was strictly that. No doubt there was communication with the outside world, but the phone would be in Jasper King's rooms.

Callie White. She was the logical answer. A level-headed commonsense woman. So before I could hunt for reasons not to confide in her, I went down the silent corridor and tapped on her door.

She was slow in answering. I was about to knock again when the door opened a crack and an eye peeked out. Then the door was immediately swung wide.

"Oh, Karen. We thought it might be someone else."

I looked around for the rest of the *we* she'd referred to, and found no one. This while trying to keep from raising my eyebrows at Callie's attire. Or rather, her lack of it. She was wearing a filmy crepe gown painted with Chinese scenes and characters. It was cut very low and stopped abruptly just above mid-thigh, and while I could not be positive, I was sure she was wearing nothing underneath. Of course, there was nothing indecent about wearing such a garment in the privacy of one's room. It just seemed out of character for Callie White, at least as I had adjudged the woman.

The *we* question was quickly answered when Callie called out, "It's all right, Rory. You can come on out. It's Karen Spain, not your ladylove."

Rory Talbott came scowling out of the closet. He too was informally dressed, although his robe reached his ankles and was far less revealing.

"Sit down, Karen," Callie invited. "Rory and I were just having a nightcap. Anything on your mind?"

"Well, yes and no."

"That covers everything. How about a brandy to see you to dreamland and stave off the fork-tailed imps?"

It was brandy again. A bottle similar to the one from

which Jasper King had neglected to pour. It seemed that I was fated to the sting of brandy in my throat, no matter where I went.

Callie made no apologies for her casual dress, thus living up to at least one impression I had of her. She took everything in stride. I would have been hard-pressed to imagine a situation that would have upset her. Whatever she'd had to drink, she held it well. Perhaps she sensed my surprise at finding her thus, and it amused her.

Rory Talbott, on the other hand, was deeper into his drinking. He eyed me morosely and asked, "How come you aren't with your flying ace?"

"Jeff Stone? I haven't seen him since early evening."

Rory shook his head. "Poor guy. He's in trouble."

"Something he brought on himself, I'm sure," Callie observed.

"Okay. So he went to hock with the wrong people. He was okay until his crate got messed up. Now he's got nothing to sell."

"The people he owes money to," I said. "Would they actually hurt him?"

"That all depends on how they decide to kill him if he doesn't come up with the scratch."

"*Kill* him! Why, that's ridiculous! Then they never would get their money."

"No, but it would be a good example to other poor devils they've got over a barrel."

"Rory, is that why Jeff has been so reckless? Walking that parapet? Going after the bear with a crossbow?"

"Probably. You see, Jeff is short on nerve normally. He talks big and lives on his dreams." Rory frowned

125

thoughtfully. "He's one of those guys who actually believe their publicity, I think."

"But it took courage to fly in the war."

Rory laughed. "You believed that?"

"Of course. He had the plane."

"That Snipe wasn't built until the early twenties—after the war was over. Besides, it's a trainer. The ones they fought with were single-seaters."

I wanted to cry. Not only that, but I wanted to take Jeff in my arms and tell him everything would be all right. It was my most complete surrender to the love I'd fought to deny. Now, rather than call myself an idiot for being so stupid, I searched desperately to justify Jeff as a person. A beautiful man! Wasn't the creation of that gorgeous, defiant image an accomplishment in itself—even more so in a person without the rock-solid common sense and stability of . . . well, of a man like Max.

Something had to be done. I told myself that, even as I refused to give mind room to what that something was.

Callie refused to be disturbed by Jeff's plight. She said, "How was the dinner, Karen?"

I paused before answering. "Confusing, to say the least."

"Did he compliment you on hauling all the decent furniture away?"

"As a matter of fact, he did."

She frowned at me musingly. "There was more than that, wasn't there?"

"Yes. He's planning to leave the castle."

Callie and Rory Talbott glanced at each other in some surprise.

"He's ready to hit back at the ones who hurt him financially. He seems to have his plans all made."

Rory leaned forward, his elbows on his knees. His look was more of a sneer than a smile. "Honey, you're way off the track. Jasper King is going nowhere on the money road. He'll keep right on sitting up there in his tower calling black white and making himself believe it."

"What do you mean?"

"It's what he did to other people that broke him. All his life he climbed over people to get to the top. He broke people, he smashed them. And he was so good at it." The boy's mouth twisted. "He killed my father."

Did that mean Rory had come up here to kill Jasper King?

As though he'd divined my thought, he said, "Jasper King is paying off, every minute of his life. Nobody needs to hurry him along."

"The others who are with you," I said. "Did Jasper hurt their parents also?"

"He hurt everybody who came in contact with him."

That made the presence of the younger group somewhat confusing. Perhaps they saw Jasper King's generosity as their right, if they blamed him for improverishing them. But there was his side of it. Was he trying to make amends through them, or was he a masochist, punishing himself by having them around him?

I said, "The death of his wife must have been a shattering blow. On top of everything else . . . losing his fortune. He must have decided the whole world was against him."

127

"The poor guy changed overnight. His close friends say he sat for two days staring into space without moving a muscle. Then he ordered them off the estate."

"How pitiful!"

"The funeral was private. Only trusted people on his staff. A photographer got a shot of them carrying Laura's casket into the family vault, and Jasper's musclemen clobbered him."

Jasper's musclemen? I could only wonder about them.

"Cancer," Rory murmured, his mind evidently going back. "No cure. Poor Laura. She was more than Jasper deserved."

It seemed to me that the poor man rated a defense. I said, "With misfortunes like that, you can hardly blame him for becoming . . . well, eccentric."

Rory laughed. "Sure. But you can't blame the people he ruined for cheering, either." His face hardened. "Personally, I'm here to watch him go down the drain."

It was a pointless argument. Callie had listened in silence, taking no side. I arose from my chair, all urge to confide in her having vanished.

"I guess I'll turn in," I said. "It's been a long day. Thanks for the brandy."

Rory Talbott yawned. "Me too." Still in his robe, he followed me to the door.

Callie's look was eloquent. It accused Rory of pointing his conquest in a new direction. But still without resentment; with amusement, rather, her ego not ruffled in the least. A strange person, Callie. I envied her. Entirely self-sufficient, she seemed to view the human comedy from the vantage point of her strength and find it enjoyable.

Rory Talbott followed me out into the corridor, where he leaned over the balustrade and looked down at the dark, foggy garden below.

"Weird," he murmured. "It's hard to get used to. As weird as the old man himself."

"Japser King?"

"Who else?"

"How well do you really know him?"

"Too well. He's off his nut, you know."

"You keep saying that."

"You've found him sane?"

"Well, possibly a little eccentric. There is something very strange going on in his tower."

"Strange? He sits up there to keep cool."

"From the sounds, he has someone with him."

I could dimly see Rory's grin in the shadowed darkness. "A woman?"

"Yes."

"Would you like a peek at her?"

"Why . . . I don't know. Mr. King's private life is—"

Rory seized my hand. "Come on. I'll show you. Even Callie White doesn't know."

I had no time to protest, even if I'd been so inclined. Rory pulled me toward the nearest stairway and up the steps past the third level. A few moments later we came out on the upper rim of the castle.

Rory's mood had brightened. He smiled into my eyes. "This is a great place to seduce a girl," he murmured. "The moon, the stars. Everything right."

I held my ground, refusing to back away. Perhaps it

was the brandy. It gave me a vaguely reckless feeling, and there might have been a moment of romance if something else hadn't gotten in the way—my tendency to regard myself as older and more mature than men even of my own age.

I said, "You're right about that, but from what I've seen, you don't need the moon and the stars. Would Ginger Wade require them?"

His amorous smile turned to a pout. "That broad! She's a pest."

"Callie White. Is she a pest too?"

"A teaser."

"You seem to have all the women here at the castle classified. Where do I fit in?"

"You're a question mark. A gorgeous question mark. Every guy around is guessing."

I would have been less than human not to be flattered by that. In fact, I allowed Rory to come closer. And again there might have been romance—if Jeff Stone's phantom face had not interposed itself.

I drew back. Rory looked disappointed.

"No chance?"

"I wouldn't say that. Please try again sometime."

He shrugged, and I almost accused him of giving up too easily. "The thing is," I said, "that this isn't what we came up here for. I don't need the moon and stars either. You could have kissed me just as easily outside Callie's door."

"You mean I tried too hard?"

"Something like that. What were you going to show me?"

He was as volatile as mercury. His grin came back, and he seized my hand. "Over this way."

As we walked, he explained. "I found out about

Jasper King's corner on ice and came up here to cool off. The cool air comes out through the tower vents."

He'd dropped his voice now, and as we approached the tower he went on tiptoe, although I didn't think that was quite necessary. With his fingers over my lips he whispered, "You'll have to stand on the parapet, but I'll hold you so that it's not dangerous. Then look down through the open vent and tell me what you see."

My curiosity overcame my fear. With Rory's arm around my waist and a hand firmly gripping my ankle, I also managed to overcome the feeling of a Peeping Thomasina, and peered down into the interior of the tower. The circular inner wall was lined with ice blocks covered with wet burlap. I could see only about a quarter of the interior; the balance was beyond my range of vision. A quarter of the room, but enough to make me feel like a fool.

I signaled retreat, and Rory eased me down. His grin awaited me. He hurried me along the walk, then turned and asked, "What did you see?"

"Jasper King's feet and ankles extending out from his chair."

"What else?"

"His phonograph. It wasn't playing at the moment."

"Now you know. It won't keep you awake nights."

"I should have known when I first heard it. At least, the possibility should have occurred to me."

"He sits up there thinking about the ruins of his empire, playing his phonograph."

"That's true, but I think there's more to it than that."

"What's the big mystery?"

"Not exactly a mystery. It's his taste in music."

"He likes female singers."

Possibly true, but what I'd heard was hardly professional. Not a bad voice, really, but one that few music lovers would pay to hear. Also, the laughter. Professionals did not laugh nor converse on records between verses.

We got back to our level, and Rory said, "I'd ask you into my place, but Ginger might cause a row."

"From what I've seen of Ginger, she certainly would."

He looked at me in sorrow. "You've proved a big disappointment to me."

"It's a problem. I disappoint so many people."

"You should adopt the broad viewpoint."

"How do I go about doing that."

"Just think of the rewards of generosity. You could have made me very happy up there, and it wouldn't have cost you anything."

"That's a way of looking at it."

"You miss a lot in life by not having the broad viewpoint."

That gave me more to think about than Rory realized. I went into my quarters and thought about it. *Had* I spent my life avoiding love? Was I, in Rory's terms, niggardly with my feminine charms? As I prepared for bed, I tried to examine my moral precepts in an objective manner. Were they rigid, or did I just have a very high passion level?

But more important, what was I missing by being the Karen Spain I knew rather than the one Rory had hoped to find up there under the moon?

The answer to my ponderings—or rather, the result of them—came after I was ready for bed. Instead of crawling in, I snatched up a robe and went to the door of Jeff Stone's bedroom.

I opened it and peered in and found him staring at the ceiling from his own bed. He slanted his eyes at me, but his expression didn't change, and I realized that if anything happened here, I was going to have to make it happen.

"You aren't asleep," I said.

"No."

"I couldn't sleep either."

If I'd waited for an invitation, I'd probably have stood in the doorway all night, so I invited myself. I approached and sat down on the edge of the bed close to him. So far, he had not moved.

I smoothed a thick lock of his hair up off his forehead. "You look tired."

"Could be."

"Did you have dinner?"

"I skipped it."

"You should eat to keep up your strength."

I realized I was acting more like a mother than a lover. In short, getting nowhere. It was now or never, I realized, and bent over and kissed him. His arm went around my shoulders, and he held me close for a few moments while he responded. Then he turned his face away.

I heard myself whispering, "I love you, darling. I tried not to, but I love you."

That appeared to interest him. He half-smiled and ran a light finger along my lips, then up the bridge of my nose and lightly along my eyebrows.

He said, "Then do it fast, precious. I won't be around long."

"You don't mean that. You're only trying to frighten me. It can't be nearly as bad as you say."

I remembered what Rory had said about the people

133

Jeff was involved with. That probably kept any honest conviction out of my voice.

He kissed me gently. "It's nothing for you to worry about."

"It *is* something for me to worry about. Exactly how much money do you owe, darling?"

"Ten thousand. It might as well be a million."

"And they won't wait? They won't give you a chance?"

"They've given me a chance."

"Then we'll run. We'll go away until we can do something to get the money."

His smile was sweet, his hand gentle as it caressed my cheek. "Angel, you wouldn't want me to do that."

"Why not? We wouldn't be cheating anybody. All we need is time."

"Baby, whatever you do, you've got to cheat somebody. That's how life is. But you don't run away. If you do, you're only cheating yourself."

Thoughts went swiftly through my mind. They concerned Jasper King sitting up there in his tower—on the bodies of those he had destroyed to get to the top. What would one miserable little picture mean to him—a man who didn't even know how many pictures he owned. And what was the greatest sin, stealing an oil painting from him or letting Jeff Stone be maimed and perhaps killed?

I saw myself entering that locked room and counting. Nine.

Mr. King, I have your inventory. Eight paintings. That's fine, Miss Spain. Just fine.

"Darling," I whispered, "we'll work it out!"

"Sure, baby."

There was an interlude beyond two friends talking

134

over a problem but short of the high passion our close proximity might have generated. I was not asked into bed, and after I got back to my room I could only wonder if I would have accepted the invitation. I told myself *yes*. Very definitely. But not convincingly. It was all very well to boast when the danger was past.

This turned out to be a time of crisis, and as often happens in such cases, it came without high emotion or any grinding of the teeth. I found myself envying fiery little Ginger Wade. When she wanted something, she took it. In short, she *lived* instead of sitting by and thinking about life and how it would be to live it.

But Karen Spain . . . ?

With that, I went back through Jeff's door and walked without hesitation to his bed.

Habit and conscience did not go completely into the discard, because I returned to my own bed just before dawn. . . .

17

The following morning I used the key Jasper King had given me and entered the rooms where his priceless art was stored. It was empty except for two straight-backed chairs in the room where the art had been carelessly placed against the wall and on the bare floor. However, the packing had been carefully done. There were seven flat wooden cases, and for long moments I stood fascinated by the names in bold black letters identifying each case: Tintoretto . . . Van Gogh . . . Rembrandt . . . Corot . . .

It was awesome, standing alone in such presence.

I did not immediately pounce upon them. First, I had no tools to open the boxes. Also, I felt that I needed a witness before opening cases of such great wealth. Still, I was loath to walk away and leave them.

There was reason to smile. This I discovered when lifting one case off the floor to lean it against the wall. Whoever had packed the treasures had a sense of humor. On the other side of the case I found the name ''Buonarroti.'' Perhaps that person had not wanted to put the revered name of Michelangelo out in plain sight.

I went down into the kitchen but did not find Callie White. However, I obtained a claw hammer, and when I returned to the third level I saw a familiar figure sweeping the corridor. I knew him only as Lee, the younger of my two assistants during the furniture transfer. It occurred to me that he would serve as my witness, so I called him to the door.

"Lee, I'd like you to help me with some unpacking."

"Right, miss."

Inside, Lee extended his hand for the hammer. "You want those boxes opened?"

"I'd rather do it, Lee. If you'll just stand by."

I was like a child under the tree on Christmas morning. Which goodie to open first? I reached for the Van Gogh, it being the smallest case.

Then stopped.

Lee looked at me questioningly.

I hesitated, not wanting to make a mistake, then asked, "Lee, were you in here while I went downstairs?"

He shook his head.

"I left the door unlocked. That was careless. Did you see anyone while I was gone?"

"I didn't even know you were up here, miss—not until you called me."

"Then you hadn't been in the corridor very long."

"Only a couple of minutes until you came. What's the problem?"

"Someone was in here. I'm absolutely sure I put the Rembrandt and the Corot side-by-side against the wall. Now they're stacked together. The Reynolds, too. I picked it up. Now it's back on the floor."

"Are any of them missing?"

"No. They count the same. Seven cases."

"Then I guess no harm's done."

He was right, of course. Still, I was upset. If someone had wandered in out of curiosity, why had they left? This was overreaction on my part, perhaps. Their curiosity satisfied, they could have wandered on. Maybe it was just my reverence for what was in those cases. I could not conceive anyone reading those names and not staying around to marvel.

"You're right," I said. "It's no problem. We'll open the Van Gogh. You're going to see something beautiful, Lee."

He nodded politely.

I lifted the lid of the case, found a heavy plywood envelope inside, and drew out a plain wooden underframe with almost a trembling hand. It was a landscaped field. The blazing color so synonymous with the mad Dutch genius radiated and seemed to light the room. The bold brushstrokes, so apparently simple that they inspired every art student to go forth and do likewise, symbolized Van Gogh's fruitless search for truth. I was enchanted, but only to be brought back to earth by Lee's unenthusiastic comment.

"It's a picture, isn't it?"

"Yes. By one of the greatest artists of all time."

"Is it worth much?"

"It's priceless."

He was obviously unconvinced, though too polite to argue the point.

I opened the Gauguin next. I'd seen a print of this one. It had been in the Samuel Driscoll Collection some five years earlier. It was a Tahitian scene, a thatched hut with two female figures reclining, naked to the waist, in the usual Gauguin style.

Lee frowned at it. "They're wrong," he complained.

"Wrong?"

"A woman doesn't look like that. It's kind of like he was practicing or didn't finish the picture."

I could only laugh. "Lee, different people get different reactions from art. That's the idea of it—to reach an emotional depth within you that you can't put into words, that you can only feel. Did a winter scene ever make you feel cold when you looked at it? Or a tropical scene make you want to take off your coat?"

He thought that over for a moment. "I don't know. I like things to look like what they are. If you actually saw the women in that picture, they'd look funny."

"You're a realist, Lee. And there's nothing wrong with that. Each of us must be his own person when it comes to art. Or anything else, for that matter."

He turned back to the Van Gogh. "The fellow that painted that one. He must have seen a real strange world around him."

"Van Gogh did, Lee. He was mad. He cut off his ear and sent it to a lady he admired."

"I could maybe figure he'd do a thing like that."

"Genius and madness often go together."

"Uh-huh. That fellow Gauguin must not have been right either."

"He was cruel and selfish. He left his wife and family and went off to paint."

"Where he could find all those naked women?"

"I really don't think that was his prime motive."

Lee shrugged.

I said, "Lee, I have some books on art if you'd like to read about some of the great paintings."

"Thanks, but I guess not. If I want to get them feelings you talk about, I'll just go out and look at the hills and the mountains. Do you need me anymore?"

"Just a few minutes."

Following through on my resolve to have a witness, I hurried with the rest of the paintings without indulging in the luxury of enjoying them. The Reynolds did hold me for a few moments as I tried to identify it and could not. It was a portrait of a child, a girl with sensitive, almost frightened blue eyes.

"This one, Lee," I said. "Here is your realism. This little girl did not trust the painter. You can see it in her face."

He studied the painting. "I wouldn't exactly say that. I think she didn't want to sit there so long. She wanted to be out playing."

His independence of thought was to be commended. "Lee, you're a dream," I said. "I just wanted you to witness the unveiling of these paintings because they're very valuable. Seven in all."

"Yeah, there's seven."

"And thanks for your time."

He moved toward the door, then paused. And perhaps it was because I'd called him a dream that he gained courage. Anyhow, he paused and said, "Miss, maybe you'd like to walk out with me some evening."

"Well, Lee . . . I . . ."

"We could go to Hempstead. That's a little town nearby. We have movies on Saturday night."

"I'd love to walk out with you, Lee. And by the way, my name is Karen."

"When?" he asked.

"Why . . . all the time. I was christened Karen."

"I mean, when shall we walk out?"

"Tomorrow night? You said there was a movie."

"I'll call for you at seven o'clock—if I don't see you before that."

"Fine."

"Then so long . . . Karen."

"So long, Lee."

He was a strange young man but thoroughly likable; given to showing very little emotion. To all appear-

141

ances, he faced "walking out" with me the same way he faced his daily work—a job to be done.

I was flattered at his invitation, nonetheless. But it soon passed from my mind in the face of my personal problems. For a long time I stared at the Van Gogh, thinking of it as a means of paying off Jeff Stone's debt rather than as a masterpiece. Then I became angry at the thought of crass loan sharks getting their grubby hands on the lovely thing. Had I been given the truth? I wondered. Could Jeff actually be killed because of money he was unable to pay back? I had to admit that I did not believe it from Jeff, but Rory Talbott had backed up Jeff's fears.

I put that aside and turned to my immediate problem. The paintings. Someone *had* investigated during my short absence. They had not seen the oils themselves. Still, the names were stenciled in bold black, and what if one or more of Jasper King's strange guests were not what they appeared to be?

I made my decision, put the canvases back into their cases, and began moving them—like a mother cat moving her kittens, it curiously occurred to me—into my own quarters, where I stowed them under my bed. I made the transfer as deviously as possible, and to the best of my knowledge, I was not seen.

I locked the door from my bedroom into the common room and then the outer door and went down into the dining hall for a drink and a few minutes' respite.

Because of the strain, perhaps, I was still unable to accept the bizarre as commonplace, even after the time I had been at the castle, and got one strange reaction after another. I paused to look down into the tropical garden and judged the panting of the monster below the caves as even more insistent, as though the beast of

Caliban's Castle was slowly wearing away the chains that held it and soon we would all answer for our presence there. Then, when I reached the dining hall and was promptly waited upon, there was the feeling of being in a luxurious restaurant waiting to serve myriads of diners but to which no one ever came. All of which was macabre, downbeat, depressing.

A person's mind can work strangely under unfamiliar circumstances. This came home to me when I realized my fantasies were merely facades to cover my real thoughts, that if I could buy the seven paintings from Jasper King, I could deliver six to Judson Conroy's syndicate and use the seventh to save Jeff Stone's life. Conroy and King were not speaking, so how would anyone find out?

Such uncharacteristic thinking could not go on indefinitely without resistance. This came in the form of flat denial. I did *not* love Jeff Stone. I had been merely temporarily attracted because of the false image he projected. Love—true love—was the solid relationship I had with Max Bowman, cemented slowly in an environment common to both of us. It was understandable that I would be drawn to Jeff. He had fought to save my life in a situation where I'd stood at death's doorstep.

At the same time, I struggled to keep my mind off the previous night. A brazen, stupid lapse during which I'd fooled myself into believing that the live-for-today philosophies of those around me had merit. By way of self-defense, I tried to justify those hours as an experiment. One had to investigate before one knew for sure. Now I knew that the surrender to the erotic, the physical delight of letting go, was not enough, even though my body still tingled with excitement at the memory.

Another important point. Jeff did not love me. He

was too busy loving himself. I'd really been only a night's diversion for him. Otherwise, I would have heard from him. He would have come to reassure me.

One aspect made me writhe inwardly—that I had gone to his bed after being lured rather than invited. As things stood, I could hardly claim even seduction. This inward struggle went on as I slowly finished my glass of lemonade, left the hall, and mounted to the third level. I knocked, and as usual there was no answer. More emboldened now than before, I knocked again and then tried the door. It was not locked; neither was Jasper King in sight.

I was not surprised by either that or the music coming from the tower. I was interested, however, in the music itself. It was that same sweet voice, but with an accompaniment of what could have been a harp or an Elizabethan lyre of some sort. The impression was of chamber music in just such a castle as this long, long ago. Sedate ladies in voluminous skirts busy at their needlepoint while being entertained by the songs of the latest traveling troubadour:

> "There was a maiden long ago
> With heart as cold as arctic snow
> As cold as cold as arctic snow.
> A hapless swain a-wooing came,
> And gave the icy maid his name
> And she did take his love—"

I never learned the fate of the ice maiden and her lover. Evidently the song did not please Jasper King, because it ended abruptly and I heard heavy footsteps from above. Fortunately, I was able to get into the corridor and close the outer door just in time.

It was opened to my second knocking, and Jasper King was so radically changed that I could not avoid reacting. He had an unpleasant growth of beard. There were cigarette ashes down the front of the dressing gown he wore, and his eyes were like two burned holes.

"Yes? Oh, Miss Spain."

"Mr. King . . . are you all right? Is there anything. . . ?"

He brushed the question aside, while still regarding me vaguely. "I'm quite all right. I did not sleep very well last night. Was there something?"

"I wanted to report on the paintings. I looked at them.

He stepped back to let me enter. "Oh, yes. Did you find them genuine?"

That seemed a curious question, to say the least. A man who had invested hundreds of thousands not sure whether or not his purchases were genuine?

"Completely authentic, Mr. King, I'm sure. And in excellent condition. Whoever packed them was very careful."

The chill from that tower of ice above the room swept down to touch me. But more than that, an emotional chilling. The room was charged with the iciness of despair. This was no ordinary man. There was an aura around him that could inspire, or frighten, or take one with him into the depths. His moods changed, but their intensity never lessened. He would be all-forgiving as a friend, dangerous as a competitor, deadly in the grip of madness.

"That's fine," he said in reply to my assurance, though it obviously made little difference to him one way or another.

"Mr. King," I heard myself saying, "after examining the paintings, I am prepared to offer you three hundred thousand dollars for the lot.''

Were those *my* words, croaked out of *my* throat? It had been purely impulsive—an attempt to shock him into showing some interest. But it had backfired. My own shock was far greater-than his.

He remained vague. ''You are still representing Conroy?''

''The Barlow Syndicate. Mr. Conroy is involved in it, but I do not know to what extent.''

''Is that a firm offer?''

''Yes.'' My fists were clenched. The nails were cutting into my flesh and I was no longer resisting the thought of *six* paintings to the Barlow people, not seven.

King said, ''I think not, Miss Spain. Not at this time.''

''Do you feel the price is too low?''

''No. I'm sure it is a very generous offer.''

Something was very wrong here. For a man whose financial back was against the wall to regard three hundred thousand dollars so casually seemed incredible. His whole appearance indicated that the money meant nothing to him. I recalled the brisk, crisp manner in which he'd told me of his plans for a comeback. Now I could hardly associate that man with the one standing before me.

''Miss Spain,'' he said, ''I hope you will stay and continue with your work.''

''I'd be glad to, Mr. King, but I cannot see much more to do. I'll make out the inventory listing the pieces and giving you my estimate of their value, which of course will be *only* an estimate.''

He was regarding me as though trying to remember who I was.

I went on. "I have no way of knowing how complete the inventory will be. I mean, this castle is a huge place, so perhaps you can help me. Where else shall I look? How widely were your treasures spread about?"

He did not reply. Then his facial control literally fell apart, the expressions changing, his face like a picture screen across which inner reflections moved in still frames. But surrealistic, a viewer able only to guess what torment was going on inside.

Then a look of indescribable sadness wiped out all else. I froze as he raised his hand and touched my hair. He caressed it gently, running his finger lightly over my profile and across my forehad. Not unlike the manner in which Jeff had caressed me. Yet, oh so different!

"Lovely," he murmured, "lovely."

Then it was as though he heard a distant voice, and he turned away. I gratefully took that as dismissal and left, closing the door behind. The one clear concept I had was that his gentle touch had not been for me, that he'd hardly realized my presence.

I hurried down the steps, wanting to find and see and be held by Jeff Stone.

For better or for worse. . . .

18

"They're looking for rain tomorrow."

"Oh? I hadn't heard."

It was Lee. I'd wandered out over the drawbridge into a beautiful day, seeking to calm my nerves after the ordeal with Jasper King. Lee was trimming a section of the hedge that bordered the horseshoe-curved road leading up to the castle. As I approached, he'd squinted up into the blue sky and then given me the weather report.

"I think they're right," he added, "so maybe we ought to walk out tonight if you haven't got anything else to do."

"I think that would be a good idea."

"Then I'll call for you at seven."

With that settled, he went back to work, leaving me to wander on. But instead of doing so, I changed my mind, went to my quarters, and took one of the paintings out from under my bed. Come what might, I was going to give myself something to file away in memory.

An afternoon with the masters.

And it was well worth the time. Projecting myself through the painted magic into the placid Tahitian villages of Gauguin was almost a tangible experience. I walked with the parasoled ladies of France and looked over Corot's shoulder as he immortalized them. The Michelangelo was unfinished, as had been a great many of that busy genius's works as the swift minutes and hours and years pursued him through the Renaissance. It was the head of a faintly sneering prince of royalty, according to the heavy gold chain around his neck and the expression. But he would be forever without shoulders, because Buonarroti had neglected to finish them before going on to something more interesting. Or perhaps the nobleman had been reluctant to pay for the work. Buonarroti feared no one, neither popes nor kings.

Callie White dropped in on me in late afternoon.

"You seem to be enjoying yourself."

"Oh, I am. So much so that I feel guilty."

She regarded the paintings strewn about on the floor. "I imagine they're very valuable."

I was surprised that a woman of her intelligence would only *suppose* it.

"Priceless, really."

"I guess anything is worth what a buyer would be willing to pay for it."

"That's about right. I made Mr. King a bid of three hundred thousand dollars for the paintings."

She gasped. "In times like these, when some people can't get enough to eat?"

I enjoyed her surprise, and parroted Judson Conroy by saying, "Callie, some people see a depression as an opportunity rather than a disaster."

"I'm sure they are few and far between."

I wanted suddenly to solicit Callie's confidence, to seek her advice and reassurance that I was doing the right thing about Jasper King and his madness, about Jeff Stone and the new problem with which I had been confronted during the afternoon. I'm sure it would have helped—at least given me the comfort of knowing I was not alone there amid the confusions and dangers of Caliban's Castle.

But I could not bring myself to seek her help, and after inviting me downstairs for a drink, which I declined, Callie started to leave.

I caught her at the door. "By the way, have you seen Jeff Stone around?"

"He went out early this morning with that silly crossbow. Honestly, I think every guest in this place is crazy." She tempered this with a quick smile. "Except you, of course."

Alone again, I repeated the futile performance I'd gone through prior to Callie's arrival, peering under the bed, finding nothing, counting and recounting. I reminded myself of a caged animal that knew there was no escape but paced back and forth in its barred space regardless. The count was my pacing. There were six cases, not seven. I'd taken them one by one from under the bed, then literally crawled under there myself. The Van Gogh was missing.

I debated my alternatives. Go straight to Jasper King and tell him what had happened? I found that I could not do that, with suspicion pointing so strongly at Jeff Stone. So what? Confront Jeff and try to persuade him to return the Van Gogh? A lifeless thing of oil and canvas which might well save his life? My decision was total evasion. I put the paintings away and got ready for my date with Lee.

Promptly at seven, he tapped on my door. I opened it and with an enthusiasm I was far from feeling exclaimed, "Lee! You look marvelous!"

He'd dressed for the occasion. He was clean-shaven and wore a sport coat with brass buttons and white ducks. An open white shirt revealed his strong, deeply tanned throat.

He took my compliment stoically. "Are you ready?"

"I'm all ready. Now, how about dinner. Downstairs?"

"My mother packed a lunch for us."

"How sweet of her!"

"I'm sorry there's no movie tonight."

"That's perfectly all right. But, Lee . . . there is something."

"Something wrong?"

"Not exactly. It's just that I don't know your last name. Actually, we were never formally introduced."

He was relieved. "When you said that, I thought you were going to tell me my necktie. I didn't wear one."

"It's too warm for a necktie."

"And I don't like things tight around my throat."

"I understand. And your name is Lee . . . ?"

"Oh. It's Lee Burgess. That's an old New England name. My family has been up here for generations."

"How wonderful. This is the first time I've met a true New Englander, except Callie White. I'm sure she's a native."

"I guess so. She went away to school, though."

I wondered if that disqualified her, but didn't ask.

Just beyond the drawbridge, Lee's chariot was waiting, a shiny black model-T Ford, old in vintage but pampered and cared for to a point that there was not a single scratch that I could see on its shiny surface.

"We can drive around to the shore the other side of Hempstead," Lee suggested. "It's nice there."

"If you don't mind, I'd like to see some of the estate.

152

I've walked to the sea over by the bluffs. Are there any roads you could follow?''

''We can take the main road down to the gate and then cut west to the edge of the marshes. If we hurry, we could catch most of the sunset there. It's real pretty.''

''Let's do that.''

The Ford purred cheerfully, and we set off with Mother Burgess's picnic basket in the back seat. We drove off down the horseshoe-curved road, which was not in too good shape once we got beyond the cultivated area around the castle. Then I saw the impressive entrance to Caliban Leach's sprawling estate. It was a massive wrought-iron gate curlicued intricately along the top, the decorations drawing the eye toward the initials C.L. in the center.

There was a small gatehouse beside the entrance. I saw this as we approached, then the four men stationed there. They were watching us, a grim group, and I remembered something that had passed from my mind—the unfriendly receptionists who had found Jeff and me at that cottage and taken us to the castle. That was the last I'd seen of them. I also remembered Rory's mention of Jasper's loyal staff. His musclemen.

They had remained loyal, but with something more than muscle. Rifles. They were armed, and poised as though they were ready for trouble, from whatever direction.

''Is Mr. King expecting a war?'' I asked.

''They're the guard,'' Lee replied. ''If you'd come by the road, they would have questioned you and phoned ahead.''

''Then they're here to keep people out, I presume. I wonder what people?''

Lee said, "A rich man like Jasper King is always a target for thieves."

"And he does have a lot of valuables in the castle."

We approached the gate. The guards eyed us but made no move. Then, as Lee turned into the side road toward the marshes, one of them raised a hand as though giving us a blessing.

Lee hurried the Ford on along the rutty road, and we came to a wide, grassy section, somewhat like a green beach on the shore of Dismal Swamp. Except, with the sun just lowering on the far side, it was not dismal. It was beautiful.

The sun was an orange crescent just above a cloud bank that ran from lighter orange into pink and finally violet at the horizon. Set against that gorgeous tapestry was an ocean of gently undulating reeds—a black foreground of an idyllic sunset landscape. It was so beautiful as to flood over my emotions and touch my nerve ends. I shivered.

Lee's arm went around me. "Are you cold?"

"No . . . oh, no. Just enchanted."

"It is pretty, isn't it?"

"I see what you mean now. You don't need paintings—not even by the masters."

"You really go for art, don't you?"

"I suffer the pangs of an uncreative person who envies those who can create."

"Maybe you never tried. If you'd paint a picture, I'd buy it sight unseen."

We'd sunk down upon the grass to enjoy the dying glory to the west. Just to make the picture absolutely perfect, chance sent a V of geese across the deepening red.

Lee's arm was still around my shoulders. It seemed

so right, so secure. He was ideal for the place and the time. A lot of Max Bowman, with just a touch of Jeff Stone. All this certainly was a new world to me.

We sat for a time in silence, and I wished time itself would stop and leave us there forever. But darkness came, and with it a quick squeeze of Lee's arm.

"Time to eat, don't you think?"

"Yes. I'm starved. I hope we can find our mouths."

"No problem."

Lee led me back to the car and took the hamper from the back seat. He also brought out a camping lamp fueled with gas. He lit it, and our picnic began.

"It won't be much like what you get at the castle," Lee said as he opened the hamper.

He was right. It was not. It was infinitely better. Fried chicken I would remember for ages. Potato salad the like of which any chef in Manhattan would have traded all his recipes. Cold lemonade in a vacuum bottle.

"I adore your mother," I said, "without even having met her. She's wonderful."

"Mom's a pretty good cook," he conceded. "How long are you going to stay at the castle?"

"I don't really know. It's all pretty confusing."

Then—and not from any urging from Lee, only his quiet, reassuring interest—I found myself reciting the whole tale of uncertainties, fears, and frustrations.

He listened with an occasional question. When I finally ran out of breath, there was a pause while he appeared to be trying to put everything I'd told him into a coherent whole.

The he said, "One thing you're doing to mix yourself up—you're trying to make sense where there isn't any."

"What do you mean?"

"Jasper King. He's mad. Anybody can see that. And you don't try to find logic in anything a madman does. He's like a jigsaw puzzle with no piece that fits any other piece."

"Then why isn't something done to help him—I mean, why is he allowed to go his mad way?"

"He's not just somebody's nutty uncle who can be parked in an asylum by relatives by just signing a paper. He's too big for that."

"Then he's just allowed to go his own way until . . . until he crashes?"

"I think maybe he'll be taken in hand. It's just that whoever tries it has to know what they're doing. And people who know what they're doing usually move slowly."

My thought was that I had a rustic philosopher here. Then I realized I was patronizing him and banished the thought. Lee rated a higher regard than that.

"Then I guess the thing for me to do is get myself out of this mess before the roof falls in."

"That might be a good idea. What we've got there at the castle can't last very long."

"What do you think of Callie White?" I asked.

"Callie's been around a long time."

"What I mean—is she taking advantage of Jasper King?"

He laughed. "Aren't we all? Every one of us is taking what we can from him in any way we can."

"But honestly. You work for your pay."

"So does Callie." He frowned before going on. "Callie is pretty strong. She has a way of taking whatever comes, without letting it affect her much."

"There's nothing wrong with that."

The gas lantern sputtered. The sunset was long over, taking with it the beauty of the marsh and the warmth in the air.

I shivered. "How about the bear that's prowling around out here? I understand he killed a man."

"Jake Felzer. It's a pretty rough bear, because Jake was a hunter. He could handle himself."

"The animal must be exceptionally vicious."

"It's a big brown, they think. They mostly stay back in the mountains, but hunger sometimes drives them lower down when the season is bad."

"I didn't know bears were carnivorous."

"You mean eating meat? They're not, generally. They live on berries and fruit and fish when they can get them. But they'll eat meat too."

"And Jeff Stone went out after the animal with a crossbow."

"Jeff Stone? He's the one you crashed with, isn't he?"

"Yes. Losing his plane was a blow to him."

"Well, I don't want to talk about your friends behind their backs, but anybody who would go after that brown with a bow and arrow is as crazy as Jasper King."

"He was challenged by the others," I said in lame defense.

"He went out this afternoon—early. I guess that was him. I didn't know he was going after bear, though. I thought it was like that crazy sword fight—some kind of a joke."

"Did you see him return?"

"No. But he may have come back."

I picked up the dishes and packed them in the hamper. "Be sure to thank your mother for the marvelous picnic dinner."

"I'll tell her you liked it."

We started back. I was grateful for the interlude away from the castle, and found myself dreading the return. It had calmed my nerves and bettered me in another way by helping me make a decision. I would leave Caliban's Castle immediately. While there was still time.

While there was still time. I was assuming that, of course. Without knowing that time had run out. . . .

19

When Lee pulled the Ford up at the drawbridge, I found that I did not want to be alone, not even for the short time I planned to remain.

"How about a nightcap?" I said. "It's really not late."

His smile showed a flash of fine white teeth I hadn't noticed before. But then, Lee's smile was seldom wide enough to show them.

"Sure. I'll stick around as long as you'll have me."

We went inside and stopped at the fountain. I dabbled my hand in the tepid water.

"I wish it were as crystal cool as it looks."

"We can't have everything, and you'd be willing to settle for warmth when zero weather hits this area in the wintertime."

"I'm afraid I'll never see one of your winters."

He took my hand, looked musingly into my face. "I guess you would get pretty restless up here, wouldn't you?"

"Do you mean . . . ?"

"For good. To live here."

He turned my hand upward and studied the palm, evidently to avoid meeting my eyes.

At that precise moment I was thinking of Jeff Stone, that Callie told me he'd gone out with his crossbow early in the morning. Evidently he'd returned and gone out again.

"You don't have to answer," Lee said.

"Oh, I'm sorry. I was thinking of that lovely sunset

—that beautiful things like that could make living up here worthwhile.''

''It isn't all we've got. There's the ocean, too.''

''How about our nightcap?''

We went hand-in-hand to the dining hall and found that waitress service had been discontinued for the night. However, there was a bar and a buffet set out for night people. Cold cuts and salads on the buffet, and an amazing array of bottles on the portable bar. I recalled the high-proof whiskey and thought perhaps Lee had passed it up in deference to me.

''I'm afraid there isn't any Kentucky corn,'' I said.

He reached for a bottle labeled vodka. ''This will do. What will you have?''

''A glass of white wine, if there is any here.''

There was—along with red and dark purple. Lee poured me a glass and helped himself to a comfortable beaker of vodka. I couldn't help but be amazed at his capacity—the ability to drink the stuff and show no reaction whatever. I wondered if strong drink was commonplace among these New Englanders.

''I have an idea,'' I said. ''Let's go out into the garden. I know a place there.''

''The Nook?''

''A little place with a table and a chaise longue.''

''I never had a drink there, but I helped build the spot for Callie White. I don't know whether King ordered it or not.''

''Well, now you're going to get some benefit from what you worked on. Only one thing—it's uncomfortably warm in there.''

It was the same temperature as usual, but for me, not unpleasant. The dropping temperatures outside had chilled me, what with my neglecting to take a jacket, so the heat was pleasant.

Also, the cozy nook amid tropical flowers, even without the moon, generated what I'd come to refer to since moving into this new world as a "reckless feeling," but perhaps it was more than that—a demand from within, biological or emotional, to become less reluctant in taking what nature offered for fear time would move in and start making wrinkles around my eyes.

Following this lead, I drew Lee down on the chaise lounge beside me. "Mmmm . . . you smell like a man," I murmured.

This was as far as I was able to go by way of invitation. If he were waiting for something on engraved stationery, he would be disappointed. He did not wait. He rose to the occasion by setting our glasses aside and taking me in his arms, and I learned through direct experience that New England men, who knew how to hold their liquor, also knew how to kiss. Not backward or overly passionate, no dramatics, just a plain, uninhibited down-to-earth kiss—in Lee's case, with the same attention to detail he would have given to trimming a hedge or fixing a piece of harness. Without asking, I now knew the rule he lived by: if it is worth doing, it is worth doing well. Evidently kissing me *was* worth doing. And he did it well. My nerve ends began to tingle in a far more exciting manner than from viewing a sunset or a painting by Vincent van Gogh.

The kiss ended suddenly. Lee frowned. "Did you hear that?"

All I'd heard was my heart beating.

Then it came again. From the stable. The neighing of horses.

"Maybe somebody forgot to feed them?"

Lee shook his head. "No. Something's scaring them. We'd better go see."

He took my hand and led me out into the square. It was very dark, the moon clouded over and the night lights hardly piercing the gloom.

The neighing continued, and now we could hear the animals plunging about in their stables.

I peered in that direction and could just make out the entrance through the gloom.

"The door is closed," I said. "There's nobody there."

"Something's wrong," Lee insisted.

We moved closer, crossing the far side of the open square in front of the drawbridge entrance.

Suddenly Lee squeezed my hand hard and whispered, "Don't move! Don't move a muscle! It will charge anything that stirs."

He assumed I knew what he was talking about. Then I saw it, and every pore in my body tightened.

"The biggest brown that ever came down out of the mountains!" Lee murmured. His arm had gone around me and was holding me close.

"Don't move," he cautioned again. "It's wounded . . . see? In its throat."

I could see quite plainly now. The great beast stood under the light just over the gateway arch. There was a shaft in its neck. It was crouched in a half-erect posture, up on its hind legs, snarling and pawing at intervals at the tormenting wound from which blood ran down its left side like a red scarf.

162

"It's looking for a place to die, I think," Lee whispered. "Animals know when their time has come. It still has plenty of speed and power, though."

"Is that an arrow in its neck?"

"From your friend's crossbow, I'll bet."

"What do we do—just stand here?"

"For now. We couldn't make the stairs if it charged."

Those were the longest moments I ever spent. I'd never seen a beast of that size outside a zoo, let alone one wounded and in agony. I fought off rising panic, the urge to run and take my chances, anything but to stand there waiting for I knew not what.

Then I forced reason to function. Lee was waiting for the beast to weaken and fall, and the only sane thing to do was rely upon his knowledge and experience—these and the strong arm encircling me. Another long few moments. Then Lee made his decision.

"It's no good. He's coming. Now, do as I say. As soon as I yell, you light out for the stairs next to the stable. I'll bait him in the other direction."

"No. I won't leave you to—"

"You'll do as I tell you," he snapped. "No arguments."

With that, he released me and threw both arms into the air. His yell rang through the courtyard as he ran, first toward the bear, and then off to the right in the direction opposite the stable. He continued to bellow defiance at the tormented animal. Its answering roar of rage stirred the horses anew, and it was a veritable bedlam through which I ran.

I reached the stairs and turned to look. The bear was moving on Lee. I had never imagined that so cumbersome an animal, let alone one wounded and dying, could travel so fast. It was gaining on Lee. I screamed a warning.

Lee reached his stairway with a scant yard to spare. The bear lashed out a taloned paw and raked his thigh. It was as though that particular microsecond became a still frame in a motion picture, holding long enough for me to realize that if Lee fell, he would be dead in moments. He moved as in slow motion then, and my eyes blurred from the strain. I blinked hard, and when I could again make out forms, it was to see the bear out of its misery, a great pile of bloody fur at the foot of the stairway. That last valiant charge had taken all its remaining strength. . . .

20

"Is it all right?"

I asked the question timorously a minute or so later. I'd come around the second-level balcony to Lee's side and was looking down the stairwell.

He was seated halfway up. "If you mean is the bear dead, he is."

I went down to Lee. "Your leg. It's bleeding."

"No problem. Only a few scratches." He would not let me tend it.

Heads were appearing in the upper archways now, but Lee paid them no attention. He went down the stairs. I followed, and he helped me climb over the huge dead body.

"I've got to check on this," he said.

He walked toward the gate. I followed. "Where are you going?"

"To find out what happened. No brown ever turned tail after being wounded."

"You mean . . . ?" I did not finish the question.

Lee stopped on the drawbridge. "You stay here. I'll let you know."

"I'm going with you!"

"All right. Maybe you'll be of some help."

We got into the Ford, and Lee drove toward the gate. I huddled beside him and remained silent. Any questions I had would be answered later.

At the gate, Lee pulled up and spoke to the guard who came forward with his rifle cradled in the crook of his arm.

Lee said, "I think there's a man in trouble. I need help for a search party."

The guard seemed more suspicious than anything else. "What kind of trouble?"

"That killer bear showed up at the castle with an arrow in its neck."

"That idiot with a crossbow?"

"I think so."

"What about that gang at the castle? Why don't you rout them out?"

"They'd be worse than useless."

The guard shook his head. "Sorry. We've got our orders. We can't leave the gate."

"You're a damned fool! Anybody invading this place wouldn't come by the gate."

"I don't know how they'd come. That's not my job to figure. We stay here." He made it final by turning back to the gatehouse.

Lee swore under his breath and U-turned the Ford back toward the castle.

"What will we do now?" I asked.

"I'll try something else."

I didn't ask what it was. We drove into the horseshoe drive, and Lee stopped near the center of the ingoing arch. "Wait here," he said.

I waited until he'd moved back and forth along the road, then started off across the lawn toward the crags to the west of the estate. I followed and caught up with him. He frowned but said nothing as he went on with his ground search. His intent was obvious. He was backtracking the bear.

We moved irregularly, seemingly at random, and I tried to make out the tracks we were following. I failed miserably, but at no time did he hesitate for more than a few moments. As we moved off the lawn and into shrub growth along the western edge of the park, it occurred to me that Lee had never mentioned his skill as a hunter.

Several times on rocky ground he became confused and ordered me to wait while he circled. But each time he moved off again confidently.

There was perhaps a half-hour of this before he froze suddenly and gripped my arm.

"Quiet!"

I heard nothing.

"Over there."

He started off at an angle to our search path, while I followed at a trot. After a hundred yards or so I heard it also. A voice faintly calling.

Lee was already kneeling beside Jeff Stone when I got there. Jeff's face was twisted in pain. I got just a flash of that look before he saw me and changed it into a smile.

"Hi, pet."

"Jeff! My God! What happened?"

"A small argument with a bear."

He was stripped to the waist, one sleeve of his shirt around his upper left arm as a tourniquet. The rest was a crimson rag thrust against his abdomen on the right side.

"That bear needed his nails trimmed." He grimaced.

"Let me see," Lee said. He shifted his position to block me out as he lifted the lower bandage and looked underneath. It was back in place before I could twist about to see, but Lee's face told me a great deal.

He said, "You stay with him. I can get the car over here. The layout isn't too rough. Don't let him move."

He was off at a run, and I lifted Jeff's head into my

lap. He was holding the smile on his face by sheer willpower, I was sure.

"That's better," he said. "I forgot to bring a pillow."

I was fighting sobs, unsuccessfully. "You fool! You utter fool! Why wouldn't you be sensible? Why wouldn't you listen?"

"We'll talk about that over a drink, precious, when I'm back on my feet again."

His eyes closed. I stroked the sweat-sopped hair up off his forehead and cradled his head fiercely in my lap.

"You . . . you beautiful fool!"

"I got him with the first arrow. It would have killed any reasonable animal, but it only made him mad. I fumbled the second shot, and he got to me."

"The bear is dead, darling. It died in the castle."

"It must have gone for the doctor. How did you two find me?"

"Lee followed the tracks. He's very good at it."

We were not really too far from the castle, and now the car's headlights appeared. Lee pulled up and got Jeff into the back seat as gently as possible, but I could see that it caused him pain. Lee drove slowly and as carefully as possible, while I sat with Jeff, holding him as though he were all the treasures of earth, which, indeed, for me he was.

"I got Callie out," Lee said. "She'll be waiting for us."

She was—in the courtyard, with a stretcher she'd gotten from somewhere. "I didn't get anybody up," she said. "We don't want that gang gawping around."

She was a pillar to lean on in times of disaster. Cool, efficient, unemotional. She and Lee got Jeff onto the stretcher while I hovered by.

"Take him up to my room," I ordered, and there was no objection.

When we'd gotten him onto the bed, Callie and Lee held a conference in the far corner of the room. Then Callie came back and said, "We think it's better not to touch him until we can get help. Lee's going for McKenzie, our local doctor. I'll go with him, because if he's out on a case, we may have to hunt for him. Heaven knows where he'd be. Just hold down the fort till we get back." She reached over and touched Jeff's shoulder. "Easy, boy," she said. "It's going to be all right."

Jeff had not opened his eyes or spoken during the trip on the stretcher, so I supposed he was unconscious. But after a minute of dead silence in the room he asked, "Have they gone?"

"Yes . . . yes. They're bringing a doctor."

He opened his eyes. "Then we're alone, precious. Sorry I dashed out this morning."

"I missed you."

He used some of his strength to squeeze my hand. "Call me Ahab," he said.

"Hush. You mustn't talk."

His eyes wandered about the room. "It wasn't in here, was it?"

"No, darling. This is my room. I came to you, remember? In your bed."

That moment of perfect rapport slipped away in a spasm of pain that twisted his face. I held him hard, wishing I could take the hurt, seeing him as a little boy who did not deserve to suffer. Even when times of great crisis are upon us, we cannot realize them for what they truly are. The realization comes afterward, when there is time only for memory and regrets.

If I had only known at the time . . .

"I was never a flier," he said. "Not in any war."

"It doesn't matter, darling. None of that matters. When you're up and around, I'll only scold you for being so reckless."

"My Moby Dick," he murmured. "My big white whale."

"Darling, you've got to be quiet until the doctor gets here."

I must have known subsconsciously even then because of my own anguished thoughts. Why had I denied what my heart told me? In times of great opportunity, we trip over pebbles when we should be climbing mountains.

Another spasm of pain as the gritting of his teeth cut into my soul.

He smiled. "The Van Gogh I took. A joke. You'll find it."

"It doesn't matter."

"Love you," he whispered.

That was the last. His hand went limp in mine, and the little-boy look came back. I knew my love was dead.

I remained remarkably calm, finding the strength somewhere. I kissed him and covered him with the lovely silk spread I should have put away as one of Jasper King's treasures but had not.

It was very quiet in the vast room. I could easily have broken down there in the emptiness, but I forced my mind to dwell on those last things he had said. The cryptic references. They had to be followed through.

I went into his bedroom, and the first thing I saw was the Van Gogh on the wall over his bed. What had been in his mind? To tease me? He could have had the painting. Gladly. Now it was not needed.

The other thing was a book on the floor beside his bed. Melville's *Moby Dick*.

That was what Jeff had meant. As Captain Ahab he had pursued his white whale. To kill or be killed, but to prove himself, to answer for his failings, imagined or otherwise.

After a while I went down into the courtyard to wait for Callie. Callie was strong and vital. She would know what to do.

They returned half an hour later with a white-haired little oldster carrying a doctor's bag, and I was able to quietly face them without tears and tell them that it was too late. . . .

21

"He meant a great deal to you, didn't he?"

This was Callie's perceptive question the following morning when she personally brought me coffee and toast.

I'd taken the sedative prescribed by Dr. McKenzie and had slept fitfully—to awaken with a headache and in the deepest depression I'd ever experienced.

"Yes," I replied. "He meant more to me than I realized."

"It's often that way. Only tragedy tells us how we really feel."

"Has Mr. King been told?"

She was slow in answering. "Yes."

"How did he take it?"

"As though it weren't important." She frowned. "The man seems far away in a world of his own."

"Perhaps he was stunned by the news. Jeff was a good friend of his."

"I don't think so. He told me to handle everything— that Jeff Stone had no relatives that he knew of."

"There has to be someone."

"I'm sure there is, but how do we reach them? His personal effects gave no clue. No letters. No diary. We took him to Sam Kenny's in Hempstead, and we'll see what develops."

"Some of the other guests here at the castle must have some information about him."

Callie grimaced. "Those heels! When they got the

word, they decided the big picnic was over and lit out. The leeches! I caught young Rory Talbott while he was packing, but he said he knew very little about Jeff's background. Rory thought he came originally from Evanston, Illinois. We'll contact the police there and see if we can locate relatives. Why don't you try to get a little more sleep?''

"I couldn't, really.''

"What are you going to do?''

"Leave. Leave as soon as possible.''

But I knew that did not mean within the next hour. I could not go back to New York with Jeff left as he was—alone, unidentified, among strangers.

So I remained where I was through that long dreary day, refusing to leave but still without the energy to form or carry out any plans.

I wandered out into the park and found Lee back at his job, hand-trimming grass along the edge of the drive. He rose from his knees and awaited me politely.

"I want to thank you for what you did last night.''

"You don't have to do that.''

"I'm grateful anyhow.'' I looked across to where two other local men were cutting grass with hand mowers. "Is this work you're doing really very important?''

"As long as we still get paid, we do our jobs.''

The closer relationship of the previous night was no longer there. Lee could be a date or he could be an employee on an estate where I was a guest, but he could not be both at the same time.

Feeling even more depressed, I went back into the castle and into the garden. Its beauty was now lost on me. The perfume of its myriad blossoms cloyed, and the heat was oppressive.

Perhaps there is something about consciously holding back grief that sharpens the mind—either that or sends it off along the borderlines between fantasy and reality. Anyhow, the feeling was strong within me that the tragedy of Caliban's Castle was not over. I should not have been able to contemplate any more horrible a climax than Jeff's terrible death; yet it now seemed a step toward an even deeper abyss. It was as though that panting monster below the caves was not finished with avenging crimes of which I had no knowledge—as though we of today were being required to pay for someone's sins of yesterday.

These were unhealthy, morbid thoughts, and I tried to banish them. I went into the dining hall, and immediately a waitress appeared to serve me. This, plus the men working outside, was the eeriest part of the whole macabre picture. It was as though they were robots, functioning to a pattern—living stage props, so to speak, that would be gathered up and stored away after the climax of the drama.

I tried to engage the girl in conversation. She was polite, friendly, eager to serve, an attitude that only furthered that first impression.

In a gesture of desperation—for me at least—I ordered a brandy, and when the girl brought it, I gulped it down like the rank drinking amateur I was. And perhaps it became my lifeline out of the morbid morass into which I'd become mired, because my immediate resolution was clear and final.

I would leave Caliban's terrible castle immediately, right now, without a single moment's further hesitation. I arose and started purposefully toward my quarters to pack.

Then, as though my decision were a trigger, the final deluge of horror came pouring down upon us.

It started with the gunfire I could hear off in the distance. . . .

22

I met Callie White in the courtyard near the draw-bridge where I'd gone to investigate the new distur-bance.

"What is it?" I asked. "What's going on?"

"I don't know. It's coming from the gatehouse. Maybe those fools are having target practice."

We went out on the bridge and peered in the direction of the gate. The groundskeepers had stopped work and were looking in that direction also.

"We could see better from the tower level," Callie said.

"Let's go up there."

It was not necessary. From over the far ridge, a company of men was approaching. As they came closer, we could see that those in front had their hands in the air. They were followed by half a dozen men with rifles. Obviously the ones in front were being herded forward as prisoners.

Callie found wry humor in the situation. "Our brave protectors," she murmured.

"But who are the others?"

"We'll know shortly."

There was ten minutes or so of suspenseful waiting before the advancing party arrived at the bridge. I recognized one of the prisoners as the guard who had spoken to Lee the previous night and refused to help in the search for Jeff. He scowled and addressed Callie.

"We didn't make a deal to hold off the law. Only trespassers with no right to come in."

With that, he stepped aside, folded his arms, and looked off into the distance. His three men did the same.

The leader of the armed group, a man whose general appearance made his gray hair seem premature, asked, "Who is in charge here?"

It was the first time I'd found Callie White uncertain. She looked at me as though asking for instructions. And perhaps it was the brandy that gave me the false courage. I asked, "Who are *you*, and what right have you to come in here armed?"

"Mark Hallman, ma'am. I'm a United States marshal come to serve papers on one Jasper King." At the same time, he took out a wallet with a metal badge attached. "Where can I find Mr. King?"

"In his quarters, I suppose. What sort of papers are you referring to?"

"We're instructed to confiscate and take possession of articles purportedly on these premises that do not belong to Mr. King. Through default on loans, he lost possession and then moved the articles beyond the jurisdiction of New York State authorities. It became a federal matter. I'm required to serve the papers."

"Are you arresting Mr. King?"

"It's a criminal matter, ma'am, but my orders are only to retrieve the unlawfully held property by whatever means."

That, of course, meant force of arms, some of which had already been used.

They had moved us back into the courtyard by weight of their numbers. Marshal Hallman said, "I'd like to get on with this, ma'am—the service. From what I can see, gathering up the illegally held property may take a while."

Callie pointed. "Mr. King's quarters are up there—in that corner."

"I guess that's where the business must be done, then," Hallman said.

I don't know why I interjected myself at this point. It was probably a mixture of fear—how Jasper King would react—and pity for his forlorn condition. At any rate, I wanted to soften the harshness of invasion upon his privacy. I said, "Please . . . let me go up alone. I'll talk to Mr. King. May I take the papers with me?"

Hallman shook his head. "No, ma'am. They've got to be served personally by an official."

"Are you saying that if they aren't served you can't take Mr. King's property?"

"It isn't his property, ma'am. The papers *will* be served and justice will be done."

"Please let me go up and bring him down."

"Do you promise that you won't merely alert him so he can hide from us?"

"I promise."

I don't know why he should have taken my word, but he did, and with some misgivings for my courage, I went to the nearest stairway and up to the third level. The outer corridor took me eastward. I reached Jasper King's quarters, and at first I was relieved to see Jasper King himself outside the door looking downward through an open archway. He already knew of the marshals' arrival, so I would not have to break the news.

It was only then that I saw the rifle in his hands—when he raised it and fired down into the courtyard. He turned and saw me. There was open madness in his face now, a twisted snarl, the look of a man who had reached the brink.

"You brought them!" he shouted. "I trusted you! You came with Conroy's plan to ruin me. Now they come with guns!"

"Mr. King . . . please!" I managed to get that out as he seized me cruelly by the arm and dragged me into his quarters. At the same time, a hail of gunfire from below announced the fact that Marshal Hallman was not a man to compromise beyond a certain point.

"I won't let them destroy me!" Jasper King roared out his defiance at the top of his lungs. "I'll fight! I'll throw Judson Conroy's hatred back in his face!"

"Mr. King! He had nothing to do with it. *I* have nothing to do with it! These men are United States marshals. They say someone else has a claim on your things. If you would only talk to them!"

"It's too late for talk!"

He began pulling me up the tower stairway. I prayed with but a single forlorn hope other than the intercession of my patron saint. King was insane. His mind was gone. Therefore he was open to abrupt changes of mood and action. Perhaps a change would come before it was too late.

I never saw the change. We arrived at the top of the stairway, where I was able to see the horror in that tower room above.

Then the whole overload of the terrible sight, heaped upon my personal tragedy, destroyed whatever bravery and courage I'd managed to piece together since arriving at Caliban's Castle. I heard my own scream of pure terror. It faded. The world went black.

I collapsed. . . .

23

There was a dream.

For a seemingly endless time there had been nightmare, dark formless things floating up from my subconscious mind.

Now, for a short interlude, I saw beauty when there had been horror. That lovely, pale creature sleeping in her icy coffin. The glow of her white gown. The faint Mona Lisa smile on her lips. All so clear in my dream state.

"The ice maiden. Beautiful . . ."

"What, dear? What did you say?"

I opened my eyes, the dream of beauty shattered in the collision of the subconscious with the reality to which I'd returned.

"Where . . . ?"

"I brought you home—here to Hempstead. You've been out for almost three days. Doc McKenzie said he was afraid of brain fever. But you're doing fine."

There was so much to learn. I struggled with questions. "Jeff . . . ?"

Callie's eyes turned sad. "There was a telegram from a cousin we located in Los Angeles. He disclaimed responsibility. We had Jeff's funeral yesterday in Hempstead. I think you should rest now."

"Jasper King . . . ?"

"Still alive, and doing all right, I guess. He shot at the marshals and then jumped from his tower. He landed in the moat, and they dug him out of the mud. He was lucky."

I wondered. Then my memory cleared, and I shuddered. "The poor, mad, miserable man! That was his wife's body in solid ice."

Callie reacted contemptuously. "He brought her up from Long Island after a fake funeral down there—right along with his other possessions. He was insane, of course, but I'll bet it was brought on by greed. He couldn't give up anything he considered his—even his wife."

"But he was generous with everyone at the castle."

"The insane are always inconsistent."

It was as good a diagnosis as any, I thought wearily. "Will you please get in touch with Judson Conroy in New York? And a friend of mine—Max Bowman?"

"We did call Mr. Conroy. He was much concerned and told us to do everything we could. He holds himself responsible for your difficulties. This Max Bowman. Where do we find him?"

Poor Max. I'd treated him so badly. I would try to explain.

But now that horror chamber in Jasper King's tower came back into my mind. Nausea followed. Lee was hovering by, and Callie sent him for Dr. McKenzie. There was another dose of sedatives. . . .

When I awoke again, it was to find Max at my bedside.

He must have seen the pain of guilt in my eyes, because he put his hand on mine and said, "Quiet. Not a word. You're supposed to rest. There'll be plenty of time later."

It was not the command so much as the tone of voice, the manner in which he spoke. Here was Max—unchanged, understanding, solid as a rock mountain.

In a sense, I was home again. . . .

I never went back to the castle. Max and Callie got my things while I stayed in Hempstead.

Lee had not intruded in the least, but while Callie and Max were gone, I asked him to take me to Jeff's grave.

"There were expenses," I said.

"Don't worry about it. We don't charge the dead in Hempstead."

It was a nice little cemetery, with stones over a hundred years old. Jeff's grave was beside that of Silas White.

"Callie's plot?"

"No. There was just room. The cemetery isn't owned by anyone."

As I stood looking down at the grave, Lee said, "I'm sorry."

"Thank you. I only knew him a short while."

"Sometimes that doesn't make any difference."

On the way back, we walked in silence for a while. I asked, "What will happen to Caliban's Castle now?"

"The same as always, I guess. It will be empty for a while, and then someone else will move in."

"Has anybody ever been truly happy there?"

"Old Caliban Leach, maybe. But in general it isn't a very happy place."

"I'll never visit it again, that's for sure."

"I don't think you could be happy anywhere near it. I mean, up here. The loneliness. You're a city girl."

The wistfulness in his voice hurt. He was so fine, so good; a lot like Max. Too proud to urge, to try to persuade.

"No, Lee. I'm afraid I could never be happy so far from . . ."

My voice trailed off. From what?

Max and I returned to New York together. Callie

183

White promised to call me when she came to the city, but I was sure she would not. There was a strong conviction within me that my northern adventure was over; the place, the people.

All but the memories.

"Why shouldnt't you have something to remember? A dream. An experience. You're entitled to it."

That from Max. After Judson Conroy gave me a thousand dollars, which I accepted. After he offered me a job in his gallery, which I refused. After Max and I had slipped into our old routine and it no longer seemed right to me. It was unfair to Max. I was not the same person who had gone to Caliban's Castle.

After I told him the whole story, leaving nothing out.

"I loved him, Max. He was gay and gallant and beautiful. He had many weaknesses. It did not matter. If he had not been killed, I would have gone with him. Anywhere."

"Would you have been happy?"

"I don't know. I never asked myself that question."

"You say he had many weaknesses. I think you're condemning yourself for falling in love with a man you would have considered unworthy of your love if he'd been described to you before you met him. You can't understand how it could have happened."

"What are you trying to tell me, Max?"

He wrestled with his answer before replying. "Let me put it this way, darling. Every girl is entitled to two loves in her lifetime. We might call them champagne love. And then bread-and-butter love."

This from Max? He surprised me. My look brought a smile.

"Honey, I'm not as unromantic as I appear to be."

"You were saying . . ."

"The champagne love comes unbidden. The bubbles tickle your nose, and it's all so wonderful . . . and painful."

That last was certainly true.

"The bread-and-butter love is a lot different. Time, habit, security—they all go into it, and it isn't bad at all, really. Far the best kind of love for the long pull."

I lowered my eyes and wanted to cry, but we were on a bench by the East River with people going by.

"Understanding, too," I said. "That's a part of it."

"A big part. Time, also. Bread-and-butter love does not intrude. It comes slowly. One day you look up, and there it is. Come to stay."

It was a nice thought. My spirits lifted. Max, strong and confident there beside me. Bread-and-butter love.

Perhaps it was closer than I suspected. . . .

THE BEST IN GOTHICS AND ROMANCE
ARE FROM BERKLEY

MORE GREAT GOTHICS
YOU'LL WANT TO READ